# THE MARIJUANISTAS OF MAUI

# THE
# MARIJUANISTAS
# OF MAUI

A SOJOURN

# PHILLIP M. SWATEK, JR.

ONE POHUE FARM

Publisher: One Pohue Farm

ISBN 978-1-0879-0471-9


1 3 5 7 9 10 8 6 4 2

To the pioneers and the early believers—William Michael Brown, Ken Pinsky, Tara Michelle, and, above all, my beautiful wife Mardi Jo whose forbearance has always amazed me.

# FOREWORD

"The illicit has an added charm."
—Tacitus, Annals

I FELT COMPELLED TO WRITE THIS BRIEF HISTORY OF my stay on the island of Maui for several reasons. As a remembrance, a personal history, it is an attempt to understand who I am now in the light of pivotal decisions made over thirty years ago. It is, therefore, something of a narcissistic indulgence. But more than that I wanted to celebrate the lives of the marijuana pioneers who undertook considerable risks to bring their crops to fruition, and therein lies the story. Now a vast industry of legal marijuana exists. Sanitized, corporate, regulated, homogenous, industrial, and thoroughly commoditized, these factories bear no resemblance to the isolated patches hidden in the heart of Hawaii's wilderness. Those plants felt the lash of wind and rain, the heat of an intense sub-tropical sun; they took root in ancient soil and flourished in an exotic landscape on the slopes of a slumbering volcano. The men and women who cultivated them were explorers, horticulturists, outdoorsmen, and visionaries. They had no safety net and did what they wanted to do in defiance of the law. Although they were by definition out-laws, these early entrepreneurs were people of conscience—model citizens, actually, for the most part. Certainly they defied convention, but many of them went on to successfully integrate them-selves into the larger community. So this is their story, and mine.

If we choose to live truthfully and fully within the moment, there probably would be no compul-sion to write. It is our lot, however, to be reflective, to share our experiences in the hope of creating resonance with our fellow human beings, sentient or otherwise. All writing is essentially mnemonic. We use it as a device to access memory, to enable our ability to reach deeply into the well of the sub-conscious. But what is truthful writing? Perhaps that is for the author and you, the reader, to decide.

SAMUEL ELIHU BINGHAM IV

# CHAPTER I

"WAKE UP. THEY'RE COMING." WILLIAM'S urgent entreaty roused me from a febrile, salacious dream in which I was erotically engaged with the beautiful Maile. I sat on the edge of the bed, and as I struggled to consciousness my firm phallus began to wilt.

"Jesus, Will, what time is it?"

"Time to move your butt Old Scout," he replied as he thrust a cup of coffee into my hand. "Don't burn your pecker." Just as muscular and broad shouldered as he had been at college, William brought to mind an image from a Greek amphora. He was the Adonis of marijuana.

Although it was September and we lived on Maui, the night air was quite cool on the slopes of Haleakala. The moon was several days past full and cast its luminescence through my bedroom window. The stars competed brilliantly, and there was no hint of matutinal light. It must have been about three o'clock.

I pulled on my jeans and a sweatshirt and shambled into the kitchen. William's wife Laura was busy making breakfast by candlelight. She stood over the stove wearing only a sweater which barely covered her ass. Her long tanned legs were firmly planted as she scrambled our eggs. As she reached up to the cupboard to grab some plates, the sweater rose to reveal the perfect orbs of a taut derriere, sans panties. "Oh Sam," she exclaimed, unfazed, "this serving is yours. Will is getting the packs ready."

I had only been on Maui a couple of weeks and was still a little shocked by the casual attitude of the inhabitants toward such flagrant displays of flesh. And I was no prude, certainly; my Ivy League education had cured me of that. Still, I was a minister's son from Litchfield, Connecticut, and I suppose a puritanical streak was genetic. My family was old Yankee stock—abstemious, flinty, judgmental, austere. They would have been appalled had they known that I had fallen in with marijuana growers from Hawaii. Ironically, some of my ancestors had come to the Islands in the 1800s as missionaries from the Yale Divinity School. Now I was becoming a heathen.

William burst into the kitchen. Laura handed him his breakfast as he sat down at the kitchen table. "Ok, Sam. My friend at the airport called to say the helicopters came in last night. They're fueling up now, so they should start flying shortly after dawn. Laura will drop us off at the first gate. We'll meet Dave and Jonas there and hike up to the big koa tree. We will have to split up." He paused and looked at me searchingly. "You'll have to go to the Hidden Valley by yourself." I nodded and began to realize the gravity of the situation. As an "apprentice" to this friendly gang of pot growers, I had heard stories of Green Harvest, the annual attack by the authorities on the Islands' "pakalolo" crop, but Will's concern conveyed its real import. A lot of money was on the line, possible arrest, even the threat of physical violence. It promised to be a stressful and exhausting day at the very least. Our patches were spread out over several miles. It would be difficult to reach them all, especially under duress. The only option was to divide our crew.

William had supplied each pack with plastic bags, duct tape, Power Bars, clippers, gloves, and a flashlight. The hope was that we would be able to harvest our pot before it was ripped off. Most of the buds would be ready or close to it—hard, sticky with resin, glistening under the late summer sun. Only a week before they had been deemed "not quite there yet." The growers had made a judgement call that could cost them many thousands of dollars.

Laura, now sensibly clad in jeans, got behind the wheel of the truck. William threw the packs in the back and covered them with a tarp. Normally we would have fired up a doobie and put some Stones on the tape deck, but today the utmost diligence was required. "So Laura, you'll drop us off short and keep driving. Don't turn around for a mile or so. If anybody asks you are looking for a lost dog."

Often we used a purloined key to access the East Maui Irrigation road system. That enabled us to park much higher up the mountain, but William felt that today we couldn't afford to have the truck identified. The extra hike would slow us down, but we were lightly laden. A silence fell over us as we drove. I rolled my window down to enjoy the rush of the cool night wind and glanced over at my old friend "Wild Bill," a sobriquet he detested and one I used advisedly. His shoulders seemed to fill half the cab; I squeezed closer to the door. He betrayed no nervousness but seemed subdued and resolute. He knew the dangers we faced, while I had only heard the stories. Laura seemed to mirror his attitude. Her face had hardened, almost spectral in the dash lights, and only partially obscured by her long blonde hair. She concentrated on the road, alert to possible traffic, a real "wheel man," the warrior princess that I first met entirely in the nude as she emerged from the surf at Makena Beach.

I was eager to relieve my own mounting tension, and to break the silence I turned and addressed William with a note of levity. "Is this more important than beating Harvard in The Game?" To my relief he broke into a broad grin and then laughed out loud.

"Do I betray my uptightness Sam? But yours is an existential question." Tugging at his beard he pretended to ponder the answer. "Hmmm.... to me our mission today is of the upmost importance. On the other hand the hopes of thousands of Old Blues are not riding on the outcome. In any event I will certainly get laid by my favorite cheerleader. Right darling?" You might get lucky was the summary of Laura's curt reply.

"Wild Bill" had been a rising star on the Yale football team until he decked an assistant coach. The ensuing controversy was widely covered by the school newspaper. I was a freshman at the time and William was two classes ahead. I was a cross-country runner and could not have cared less about the fortunes of the footballers, but I was intrigued by the story. William conducted his own defense before the Disciplinary Committee, and in the end was acquitted of assault charges although everyone agreed that his football career was over. He became something of a hero to the left leaning student body when he denounced the coaching staff as "authoritarian fascists, cretins, and repressed homosexuals." The real issue, I later found out, was that the coach had referred to the bearded W as a "hippy." Wild Bill spent his summers working heavy construction in Honolulu as a proud member of local 368 and took particular offense at that demeaning remark.

Laura began to slow down as we reached our drop off point on the Hana Highway. A hundred yards ahead we saw three quick flashes of light. Dave and Jonas, W's partners, had already arrived and were signaling that all was clear. In this pre-cell phone era William gave brief instructions to Laura. "Come back at dark-thirty. Only stop if you see the flashlight signal, otherwise keep driving. If we aren't there make a few passes, and if we still aren't there...." Laura brought the truck to an abrupt stop.

"Be careful William." Her face was grave. "Please remember your family and don't do anything rash." She knew her man.

"Careful is my middle name O wife of mine." He leaned over to give her a quick kiss. "Come Samuel, once more into the breach! You do remember your Shakespeare? Henry V." We jumped out, grabbed our packs, and Laura quickly took off down the highway. We whispered good morning to our comrades, scaled the gate and began our hike up the mountain in utter silence, ever alert to a possible ambush. After all if the authorities could afford to fly half a dozen helicopters, positioning a few men on the ground would be a reasonable expense.

Although the packs were light, we had worked up a good sweat after an hour's march. The eastern sky was beginning to reveal the coming dawn as the stars slowly dimmed; a thin brush of cirrus clouds floated high above a solitary bank of cumulus that rested just above the horizon. Now that we were higher up the mountain, the ocean lay before us, still black in contrast to the rapidly brightening sky. We took our packs off and rested beneath a huge lowland koa tree. Above us, the leaves began to dance in the trade wind's first gentle breath. It promised to be a clear and excruciatingly hot September day.

Our little posse relaxed a bit as we passed around a thermos of coffee. It had been an uneventful expedition so far. "They always seem to know when the pot is ready don't they?" said Jonas with a serious mien.

Dave turned to him in mock exasperation. "Well of course they do! They make a fortune from stealing our pot. They let the hippies work all year then rip it off a week short of perfection. Fuck they make a lot of money. The bruddahs in

7

Keanae told me that they fly it directly to the Big Island for processing. They off load it at Lincoln Makuakane's ranch in Waimea, dry it and trim it there, then take it to Oahu where the Syndicate distributes it. And who's going to fuck with Makuakane?" I, ever the innocent, wanted to know who this fellow was. "Basically the head of all criminal activities in the state. Gambling, prostitution, drugs, extortion, you name it. Even the Japanese give him a slice of their action. He started out as a vice cop in Honolulu and bullied, threatened, cajoled, bribed, and even killed to consolidate his empire. Of course he was politically well connected, contributing generously to various Democratic candidates—at all levels."

William broke out a bag of buds and began to roll a joint, elaborating on Dave's discourse. "This is the way it's always been in Hawaii, Sam. A collusion of crooked cops, politicians, criminals, shady lawyers, developers, commissioners, bureaucrats, union bosses, ordinary thugs, and a legion of sycophants and toadies. And the haole elite looks the other way. They make their money the old fashioned way—banking, shipping, businesses with interlocking directorates. They belong to the Outrigger Canoe Club and send their kids to Punahou—my alma mater as you know. And we, well I guess we're just a bunch of pirates." He twisted the ends of the joint and then carefully lit it, slowly roasting the tip like a fine cigar before drawing the first toke.

As the doobie was passed around I laughed inwardly as I recalled when I first met William Kainalu King in college. Intent on buying my first "lid" of pot, I had been brought to his room by my freshman counselor of all people. I would soon find out that W ran the largest marijuana network on campus, and that a few counselors, lecturers, and assistant professors were part of it. I was initially nervous in the presence of such a notorious campus legend, but he quickly put me at ease with a friendly grin and a glass of hot sake. "So Scout, you must want a sample?" He reclined on a mattress wearing a pair of surf shorts and a garish unbuttoned aloha shirt. When I told him that I had never smoked before, he gaped at me in unaffected disbelief. "Oh well," he said recovering, "this will be an honor, breaking the hymen as it were. Star, could you fire one up?" Starshine, his famously beautiful girl-friend, was loosely wrapped in a sheet and had the wild, predatory look of a panther. She tossed back her long black hair, and the candlelight empha-sized her high cheek bones and aquiline nose. The clinging fabric outlined her perfect small breasts and erect nipples. The musk of sex was heavy in the air, commingling with the burning incense. She handed me the joint, looking at me with pen-etrating, unblinking eyes. I felt possessed, utterly bewitched by this enchanting mystagogue. There were no women like this in Litchfield, Connecticut. I coughed, of course, but I remember later feeling buoyant and happy on the walk back to Bingham Hall. I was liberated. I was hip!

My revere was suddenly broken as William put a hand on my knee and issued an urgent command. "Listen!" I heard nothing at all, and then, faintly, what sounded like the beat of distant drums. The sound grew, almost imperceptibly at first, before becoming a distinct and resonant pulse. "Fuck! Here they come." I must have looked bewildered. "The helicopters Sam! Green Harvest! And I bet they're coming our way." We all jumped up. "Dave, you and Jonas head out to the West Ridge. I'll take the patches above the EMI road. Sam, old friend, you are going to have to go it alone, but you know the way to Hidden Valley. Follow the pig trail, then drop into the stream bed. There's not much water in it now. You'll recognize the entrance to the patch. Remember it's behind a big hapu fern. Take everything, most of it is ready anyway. They have forward looking infrared, so conceal yourself under the ledge if you think you are exposed." The sun had not yet cleared the horizon, but the eastern sky was turning a brilliant yellow.

Dave was a Vietnam vet, and he recognized the sound all too well. "Yep, Hueys," he said adjusting his binoculars. "And it looks like a

Hughes 500 as a spotter. Must be my karma to be on the receiving end of this bullshit. Where's my M-16 when I need it?"

Jonas, the gangly hippy, rose to the bait as Dave knew he would. "David, you know that they would like nothing more than to have us shoot one down. Then they could justify any sort of repression..."

"I know love brother, I'm just jerking your chain. Peace be with you. Now let's hit it."

William adjusted his pack and looked me in the eye. "Sam, I've got a long way to go. We'll meet back here around dark. Be careful." By now the deep bass notes of the helicopters' engines were accompanied by the thwop of rotor blades and the buzzing of the smaller spotter copter. William vanished down a trail as I headed in the opposite direction My "apprenticeship" had only begun a few weeks earlier when, at W's insistence, I had fled an unhappy affair in Boston and flew out to Maui to lick my psychic wounds. I had been to "Hidden Valley" several times and was confident that I could find it, but nothing in my training as an Eagle Scout had prepared me for an airborne assault. The approaching phalanx was ominous and minacious. The dreadful noise, even from miles away, was visceral and deeply unsettling. I felt a surge of adrenalin and my quick walk turned into a fast trot. The sun had risen, but the shadows were still deep in the narrow valley that

I was ascending, and I stumbled several times in my haste. I abandoned the trail and slipped down into the stream bed. A moment later a huge black boar with scimitar like tusks crashed out of the brush ahead and scrambled up the opposite bank, terrified by the onslaught of the Valkyries. I gathered myself and pressed on. With every passing moment the sounds grew, reverberating off the side of the mountain and filling the valley with a disorienting cacophony; they seemed to come from every direction at once, and my vision was limited by the canopy of trees. Suddenly the noise was deafening; a Huey passed directly overhead, not more than fifty feet above the trees. Now I was truly frightened. I ducked under a rock ledge as the copter slowly continued up the valley, a malevolent mechanized predator searching the once peaceful forest. When the din began to recede, I resumed my short dash to the patch. I had to burrow my way through a tunnel in the stag horn fern whose vines were woody and dense. I emerged into the patch and—mirabli dictu!—the plants were still there. Thirty gorgeous eight foot females in five terraces. Green and gold, they glistened with resin, and sparkled with the first rays of the sun. They had been staked up but still sagged under the heavy weight of the kolas.

From the uppermost terrace I could look up the narrow defile. A single Huey seemed to be hovering a half a mile away. Suddenly an angry buzzing seemed to come out of nowhere. I quickly hopped down the slope and took cover in the rabbit hole tunnel. The spotter chopper flashed overhead and made a long climbing turn to the east, banking to look down the valley before disappearing several ridges over. The main force of Hueys had split up and the spotter was trying to find new targets. Thirty seconds or so went by before it returned, again describing the same arc. The search was tightening; several more passes confirmed my suspicion. I knew that I had about a half a minute each time when I could not be seen. I took out my machete, waited for that narrow window of opportunity, and sprang up, hurriedly slashing at the bases of the plants on the top tier. I dragged them to the bottom of the patch just in time. I repeated the process until I had harvested fifteen plants, too many to drag through the tunnel. I threw them over the stag horn hedge. As I emerged for the fourth time, I noticed that the upslope Huey was much closer, still hovering, its engines now a roar. I realized then that other growers had been working above us. My heart was pounding; I tried to calm myself with deep breathing, but I had to act with alacrity. I had only a few minutes at the most. I cut every remaining plant, pitching them outside the patch. The noise became so loud that I couldn't locate it. Nearby trees began to shake wildly. A shadow blotted out the sun. I was almost under the helicopter! I vaulted over the vegetative enclosure, lassoed the plants together with a rope that I had prepared and began to run, dragging the sheaf of marijuana behind me. I found a pig trail which made the going easier. I was afraid to look back, but after a quarter mile, I was gasping for breath. I turned, expecting to confront pursuers, but there were none. I sang a soft miserere mei deus. I could see the hovering Huey; it would be apparent that the plants had just been harvested. If they followed me on foot, they would surely catch me, encumbered as I was by a hundred pounds wet of pakalolo. I was certainly not in the same shape as I was when I ran cross-country at Yale. Fortunately, I was near a small, familiar cave where I stashed the bundle, covering the entrance with branches of deadfall. Only the smell could give away the hiding place. Now I limped away, having re-injured a bad knee. My t-shirt was thoroughly soaked and blood ran from a gash in my forehead, the result of a collision with low hanging tree branch. I positioned myself a scant fifty yards above the cave, although I had not given any thought to how I could possibly protect my hard won treasure.

As time went by my adrenalin subsided, and I was overcome by a deep exhaustion. The trade winds began to blow steadily, and I shivered even as the day grew hotter. The helicopters were still flying in the general area but at a much greater distance. I ate a Power Bar, leaned back against a tree, and must have dozed off, only to be startled awake by the distinct sound of guttural voices. Instantly alert, I crawled higher up the side of the ridge and peered down into the stream bed. Two guardsmen—or cops wearing jumpsuits—were sitting on a log eating lunch. They were close to the cave but upwind. Their conversation was inaudible, but I could hear an occasional laugh. They seemed to be in high spirits, even giddy, at the prospect of their new found fortune. I recognized them as "mokes,"—thick set, dark individuals, at least part Hawaiian, who spoke a sort of patois called pidgin. Although I had only been in Hawaii for a few weeks, William had been quick to instruct me in the identities of the various social groups who made up local society. I gathered that mokes were to be feared, although he seemed to be genuinely friendly with many of them. Of course he was dark skinned, grew up in Hawaii, and could engage them colloquially. I, on the other hand, was a mere "haole," painfully Caucasian and unable to understand much of what they said.

I'm not sure what motivated me to do what I did next. I know that I was angry at the casual theft, the overwhelming display of military force, the brutal mechanism of oppression. As an apprentice I would only receive a small share of the harvest, but none the less I had a proprietary sense of ownership, and the thought of a couple of goons discovering the pot was too much to bear. I crawled down to the cave, pausing to catch any sound of alarm from the picnicking mokes, now only yards away. Their conversation was distinct. I carefully, silently, removed the deadfall and extracted the tightly bound bale of marijuana. I felt light headed with apprehension. Balancing the load on my back, I stole away. Fortunately the trade winds had picked up, masking my hurried departure. I achieved the ridge top and started down toward the rendezvous at a brisk pace. But now I was exposed, and although the helicopters seemed to be at a safe remove, I knew that could change in a moment. I felt vulnerable and picked my way cautiously through the tree line. I decided to rest, knowing that I had plenty of time to make the meet-up before dark. My rest was short-lived however, for no sooner had I kicked back when the growing mechanical beat of two choppers signaled their approach. I felt fairly secure in my hiding spot and watched as they passed a couple of hundred yards to the west, dangling what appeared to be veritable haystacks of marijuana. They circled, hovered, and discharged their cargo which was hastily packed by a ground crew into a much larger double rotor helicopter parked in the middle of a pasture.

A few minutes later it took off, heading east, quickly gaining altitude.

Now, for the first time that day, it was quiet. Exhausted, I made a pillow of my sweatshirt and fell into a deep sleep. When I awoke it was very late in the afternoon, but I made my way to the koa tree well before dark. David and Jonas were already there, slumped over, dejected, a single plastic trash bag between them. They were startled by my approach and then smiled wearily. David jumped up and clapped me on the back. "Damn, Samuel, you pulled it off! All we got was the Sweet Sixteen. Fuckers ripped off everything else. You done good, Preacher. Maybe saved our collective financial asses." We were silently smoking a joint when William arrived. He had a couple of bags tied to his backpack and wore a gloomy countenance.

"Well, they got most everything above the EMI road. I saved Little Shiva, but that's it." He suddenly brightened when he saw what I had done. "Sam you're a hero! I'm so proud of you." I gave a synopsis of the day's adventure which required no embellishment. The others listened attentively, and I basked in my new found status, carefully maintaining a long face in keeping with the general mood. My New England family was only capable of meeting out occasional exiguous praise, and I was thrilled to be so esteemed by "Wild Bill," my spiritual big brother. "I do believe you deserve a promotion, Samuel."

"A promotion?"

"Yes, to full partner. Next year."

"Next year?" I was incredulous. I felt my law school education slipping away.

"Yes, and we are going to start early, this winter. Well, saddle up guys. Laura will be waiting."

# CHAPTER II

THE MEAGER HARVEST CERTAINLY CAST A PALL over all our lives for the next couple of months. The new addition that Laurie had planned for the house was put on indefinite hold. The previous winter's ski trip to Banff was not to be replicated. The beat up truck would have to serve another year. The general mood began to lighten by Thanksgiving, however. The winter surf on the north shore was now in evidence, and Dave and William were palpably excited by the prospect of the new season. Apparently the omens were favorable. I was told that winter in Hawaii often brought torrential rains, sometimes for weeks on end, but the weather in December was beautiful. The occasional rain shower brought forth a verdant deep-green to the Upcountry pastures which had been a sickly yellow in the summer. The trade winds had lost some of their bluster, replaced entirely on some days by gentle Kona—southerly—breezes.

I would often accompany the guys to Ho'okipa— there was nothing else to do—and watch as they danced with the waves. William exhibited a leonine grace while David, the determined bulldog, demonstrated a more compact and belligerent style. Laura would sometimes surf, too, but often relegated herself to playing in the tide pools with Stryder, their indefatigable two and a half year old. Of course W would spell her—the good husband—and she showed as much prowess in the water as any of the regulars. This was in an era when accomplished female surfers were rare, and indeed unwelcome in some places. Her emergence from the surf always occasioned more than a few longing stares, but for the most part she was respected as "one of the boys." My incongruous presence was easily explained; I was a "visiting cousin." This seemed to reassure the more skeptical locals, some of whom were hostile to mainland haoles. Of course I did attempt to surf, and with William's patient instruction I became capable of tackling "Pavilions" on smaller days. Gradually I took on some protective coloring. My arms and back became a little sinewy, and a light tan replaced my New England pallor. These days were idyllic. There wasn't much money, but there was always plenty of beer, and someone usually had some pig meat or a fish to throw on the barbeque. This was a time before the windsurfing invasion had taken hold or the influx of hordes of wealthy mainlanders. The local culture was still very much in evidence. Around the fire guitars and ukuleles were pulled out along with a fresh six-pack, and the singing and playing would often go on well into the night.

It was these gatherings that really allowed me to integrate with the locals. I had spent years studying the cello; indeed I had played in the Connecticut Youth Symphony, but in college I had taken up the electric guitar at Will's urging. I found that I had a remarkable ear for Hawaiian slack-key, which often used non-standard or even secret tunings. Aki acknowledged me one night, flashing a broad smile as the flames flickered over his dark face. "Hey haole boy, you pretty good." He held up a beer in salute. I returned his salute in kind, and we both drained our Budweisers. I think now it was the first time I caught Maile's attention, although I only had fleeting glimpses of her, partially hidden as she was in the shadows on the periphery of the party. I was smitten at that moment, and if I wished that our lives would someday become entwined, I could only dismiss such a thought as hopeless fantasy. She was at the gathering but not of it. Her bearing was uncon-sciously regal, accentuated by her height. A mane of black hair fell to her waist and framed big brown doe eyes that had a slightly Asian cant. I would find out later that she was an exotic blend of Hawaiian, Tahitian, Chinese, and haole.

# CHAPTER III

SHORTLY BEFORE CHRISTMAS WILLIAM RECEIVED A call from Madeline, a big time New York pot broker and his most reliable dealer in the city. She hadn't heard from him and wondered if he was coming. Was he ok? Her clients were tired of Columbian and were clamoring for "Maui Wowee." W explained that he had experienced a "bad year," but she urged him to bring what he had, and she would, as usual, make it worth his while. Since pot was difficult to move on Maui, the New York market had absorbed most of William's harvest for the past several years. He felt that it was important to keep that connection going, and besides we were all broke. David and Jonas were happy to turn their pot into money, so they added their few pounds to ours, and Aki's crew threw in what little they had. In the end we cobbled together thirty pounds. Will invited me to tag along, affording me the opportunity to engage with my east coast relations for the holidays. On the day of departure we went to the airport early, had our luggage inspected and tagged, and then returned home to replace the clothing with carefully seal-a-mealed pounds of pakalolo. That evening we presented ourselves at the United counter in coat and tie, first class tickets in hand. The disguise was perfect; we were treated with all the deference due to Hollywood celebrities. The flight was uneventful, fueled by a great deal of champagne happily served by the flirtatious flight attendants. The moment of truth came at JFK when our luggage appeared on the carousel, not a narc in sight. We grabbed the bags, hailed a cab, and rode that splendid rush into the throbbing metropolis.

---

Madeline occupied a beautiful brownstone townhouse in the West Village. A beefy doorman answered our discreet knock, and his stern Irish demeanor immediately softened when he recognized William. "It's good to see you again Billy me boy. The Lady is expecting you. And this must be Cousin Sam!" He warmly shook both our hands. "Well then. Welcome. Come join the party." We were ushered into an exuberant soiree that occupied the entire downstairs floor. Junk bond brokers, gallery owners, musicians, politicians, actors, models—the demimonde of New York night life—were talking animatedly over the frequent eruption of gay laughter. A waiter in black tie circulated with flutes of Dom Perignon, while another offered lines of cocaine on a silver tray. I recognized a famous starlet and nudged William, but he reminded me to be cool. Within half an hour I was thoroughly buzzed and found myself discussing the current state of the music industry with a notorious British rock star and his sluttish girlfriend. W had seen to it that a few joints were circulating, and he seemed to be enjoying the company of several slinky model-types with deeply revealing decolletage. If this was the underworld life, I was all for it. I was concerned, though, that such an enterprise would attract the attention of the police. When I mentioned this to William he just laughed and said, "Sam, you are so wonderfully naïve. Always remain that way old friend, it's part of your charm." I must have looked puzzled. He paused, as if he could hardly believe how dense I was. "Sam, Madeline employs two NYPD detectives to babysit these affairs. Does anybody look worried?" I had to admit that nobody seemed to be in the least bit uptight. Just then the Irish bouncer appeared and announced that we could now go upstairs to see "The Lady." Apparently clients were summoned from the party one at a time to do their business. We went up a broad flight of stairs where a guard opened the door to a cavernous bedroom. Madeline, a large woman, reclined before us on an enormous circular bed, propped up by satin pillows. In front of her were bags of white powder, pills, marijuana, and stacks of rubber-banded hundred dollar bills.

"Ah William, my love," she crooned, holding out two arms and offering a cheek to be kissed. After circumnavigating the formidable boundaries of the bed, he clasped her hands and gave her a warm peck. "I trust you are having a good time." She gave a sly look. "Penelope has been asking after you." She turned to me. "And Sam, welcome. You are evidently enjoying my hospitality." I bobbed my head up and down to signal the affirmative. I was very stoned. "So William, you said in your message that you could only scrape together thirty pounds."

"Sadly, yes. It was a bad year."

"Fortune is a fickle lady, as well I know.... So that comes to $84,000, does it not?" William nodded. "It will take me a couple of hours to put that together." She pouted coquettishly and then summoned a minion to her side. "Donald, run up to Upper East Side and collect the balance of the debt on that coke deal." He jumped up and left without a word. "Sometimes William I grow a little weary of this....this pretense....these people." Madeline fell back on her bed, seemingly exhausted.

"Maybe you need a vacation, Mad. Come out to Maui and visit us for a couple of weeks."

"This operation would fall apart in a moment." She paused. "Unless you would be willing to take over for a bit. I'm serious."

"Darling, my scene would fall apart. And besides, your clientele is drawn to you by the character you portray, with all the theatrical embellishments."

"So, are we condemned, then, to ride on this merry-go-round forever?"

"We need to develop some legitimate business alternatives."

"You know that I've tried. My clothing line for big women has gone nowhere. And if anything, the fashion world is far more corrupt than ours. I don't trust any of my suppliers or retailers. They'd rip me off in a heartbeat if they could." She seemed pensive. "Well enough about my problems. Give me two hours."

"I'll be back with the pot. It's as good as ever." Madeline was disinclined to move from the regal position in which she had ensconced herself, so William leaned over and once again gently kissed her on the cheek. On the way out we indulged in some more champagne—it was an excellent vintage—and a couple of thin lines of coke; it was uncut. The December night was bracing but not bitter. A neighborhood cafe was still gamely seating patrons on the sidewalk, so we stopped for a bite to eat and flirted with the aspiring actress-waitress who was rewarded with a large tip. Over Irish coffee Will told the story of meeting Madeline years before. He had been introduced to her by "Z," and they did their first deal that night. When Will sobered up he realized that he was short five grand. In the early dawn he ran back across town and arrived panting at Maddy's door. After he explained himself locks were unbolted and he was ushered in. She heard him out, they ran through the numbers, and she literally fished out a 5,000 dollar brick from her bosom. Her pretense of being an English aristocrat was betrayed by a soft Texas accent which William detected immediately. As she made tea Madeline told of her upbringing in a little Texas town and her fierce determination to make real money. She started out by smuggling hash out of Afghanistan, a few keys at a time, which was a risky proposition for anyone, especially a female. She grew her empire over the years and always "dealt everyone straight." She was self-made and proud of it. That was the beginning of their business relationship and a profound friendship which underlay it.

We retrieved the pakalolo from the upscale bed and breakfast where we had rented a couple of rooms. By now it was two in the morning, but the energy at Madeline's, far from waning, had only intensified. This was the fabulous side of New York that heretofore I had only heard about. In our college days we patronized dive bars that smelled of stale beer and ammonia and crashed in student apartments that were merely tenements.

We walked through the party crowd carrying a couple of suitcases without attracting a single remark. W ascended the staircase and a few minutes later was at my side with a single attache case. "Ok, Sam. This is the distillation of our efforts. Let's blow this joint." As we were making our way out, Donald appeared and slipped William a note which he read carefully several times before breaking out a large grin. "Tell Miss Penelope that tomorrow night will be....lovely!....and to bring a friend for Sam here." Donald bowed slightly, unable to suppress a small smile. W had been upbeat but a little tired, and now he seemed ebullient. "Let me tell you Sam, this woman has got it goin' on! She loves to party. And don't you worry about her friend. She only hangs with the beautiful people. P does small sales for Madeline—you know, grams and zs for visiting rock bands. She also transports money around town. She has a black gamma mink coat with specially tailored pockets to conceal the dough." Plainly, for William, the city was a much needed tonic to compensate for the brutal labor and tedious domesticity that he suffered much of the year.

The next evening we stood at the appointed street corner, resplendent in black tie, courtesy of a professional costumier friend who worked on Broadway. At precisely eight o'clock a white Lincoln stretch limo pulled up to the curb. The chauffeur, a sturdy Italian fellow, opened the rear door. I recognized Penelope because she was wearing her trademark mink, and possibly little else. Annie, her friend, was attired in a black silk cocktail dress, sans bra. Both were incredibly beautiful in that artificial, overwrought New York way; I had already developed a preference for Maui girls. Before introductions could even be made, William and P indulged in a prolonged kiss. Her coat rode up to her upper thigh as she turned in her seat to engage him. I caught a fleeting glimpse of her crotch, barely sheathed by a pair of skimpy panties; she emanated feral heat. As we pulled away from the curb, Annie popped the first bottle of Dom which had been chilling in the ice bucket. The aperture between our compartment and the driver slid open, and Tony announced that he would hold the coke because he was jake with all the cops. All we had to do was tap on the partition.

Penelope had planned an ambitious agenda which called for making the rounds to a number of parties, carefully ordered, beginning with a somewhat reserved gathering at an art gallery in Soho and culminating in wild dancing at at disco rented for the night by a rich client. It was holiday season in New York, and the whole city was committed to partying. To sober up we did a turn through Central Park, standing on the seat and sticking our heads through the moon roof, singing along with the Rolling Stones, P drinking directly from the bottle that she clutched in one hand.

By three o'clock I was reeling, feeling a little ill, and glad to be dropped off at the b and b. I wouldn't be getting laid, but it was just as well. All I wanted to do was to take a hot bath and lie down.

As I bade farewell, Annie slithered in close to William and, leaning across him, a hand on his thigh, feverishly kissed Penelope. I would not see William until the next afternoon.

———

When he reappeared, looking thrashed but happy, I could not suppress a certain jealousy which I must have betrayed by my somewhat caustic inquiries regarding his egregious solecism. "Now come on Sam. You were barely awake, and those women had their claws out. Literally." He laughed at a secret remembrance. "And besides, you're a sentimental fellow. You're falling in love with Maile, aren't you? So spare me a predicatory lecture." I acknowledged what he said; I couldn't remain in a state of pique. William was just too full of animal spirits, of bonhomie, and honest affection for me.

"But Will, you're in love with Laurie. You told me that she is the light of your life. And she makes these women, these voluptuaries, as attractive as they are, look like mannequins. Does she know about these.... indiscretions?"

"Samuel, let me tell you the facts of life. You've never been married. You have to have a piece of strange now and again. And after all it's Christmas!" A ridiculous non sequitur. He laughed again. "Besides, have you ever eaten two pussies at once? I thought not. The Chinese believe it's an elixir, a formula for longevity." He burped and slumped into a chair. "But enough is enough. Time to go home. I'll book us a couple of first class tickets. Let's go surfing."

# CHAPTER IV

WE WERE WELL MET UPON OUR RETURN. Dave and Jonas, as well as Aki and his crew, were delighted to have a little money, although it was obvious to all of us that our meager harvest would make for a tough year. Our partners were not sophisticates, and our tales of New York left them spellbound and a bit awestruck. Of course William was careful to eliminate any ribald references in the presence of Laurie. In the telling he reduced his amorous adventures to mere frat boy hi-jinks, and chose instead to emphasize cultural diversions like our night at the Metropolitan Opera—a splendid production of "Cossi Fan Tutti."

As W often pointed out, I had never been married, but in observing W and L, I was able to draw some conclusions about the connubial state. In no relationship do we know the complete person;

certain facets are revealed to different individuals. It was hard to imagine that Laura did not know her man, but she wisely chose not to ask questions which would have put him in an awkward position. She married a pirate, after all, obeying her own predilections, and no doubt her own needs were well met. Then, too, little Stryder was the object of their obvious shared affection. I felt that a happy compromise had been struck between them. Back then all marriages seemed to me a little odd (and frankly still do), but in examining societies in general, anthropologically speaking, we must conclude that the institution is normative. What makes two people splice their lives together? A biological prompting? Narcissism? W and L seemed at times like Norse gods—an appropriate pairing. But what of us lesser beings? My failed relationship with Naomi had been my impetus for fleeing the East Coast. Did I "love" her, or was her fierce intelligence something that I felt lacking in myself? Was admiration more important than "love?" And was love, a mercurial passion, the best predictor for success in a relationship? Surely a firm foundation had to be built on something more substantial.

William had known rich girls at Yale, but he shunned them, finally, as "spoiled princesses," and "daddy's girls." Rather he seemed to be drawn to singers, actresses, dancers, artists, and poets—all beautiful, needless to say. He told me once of visiting a girlfriend's parents in Greenwich and how he felt the whole time like he was being interviewed. (He had borrowed a blue blazer for the occasion). The old man, a Yalie, obviously admired W's studly qualities—they talked about the football team's prospects—but Mother's full endorsement was seemingly withheld by W's less than patrician background. Then, too, the unasked question in the air must have been are you fucking our daughter? The answer, of course, would have been certainly, yes sir! And a nice little piece she is, especially after a bottle of sake and a good joint.

My own collegiate experience was greatly enhanced when I was enlisted by William to join his pot business. I rose quickly in the ranks and was awarded the sophomore class as my exclusive territory. I was transformed, lifted out of the genteel poverty of my youth. An expensive black leather jacket replaced my camel hair coat. I grew my hair out and affected sideburns and a mustache. Motorcycle boots replaced my wing tips. My faithful cello became an electric guitar. More than that I had money, which allowed me to take ski trips to Vermont, spend a spring break in Bermuda, and above all to enjoy the willing company of long haired, polished college girls. By the end of my second year, my mother claimed "not to recognize me," while Dad lectured me on the virtues of abstinence with a patrician condescension. My family has lived in western Connecticut since the 1600s, never lured by the romance of the frontier. My mother proudly traced her lineage through the D.A.R. and attended monthly meetings with others of her persuasion until she died. As an only child I was invested with the ambitions of my parents who, to their credit, believed in the value of higher education. Yale was thought to be a conservative choice, although they worried about the increasing number of Jewish students who were enrolled there. Soon I gave up on visits home despite the proximity of Litchfield to New Haven.

After William graduated school seemed a lot less interesting. I finally received my own diploma and found a job in a music store in Boston. My meager salary was supplemented by my work as a musician. I played in several bands over the years and enjoyed some local success but never got a recording contract. During that time I kept in touch with William and followed his checkered career. He was a lifeguard on Oahu for awhile and then eventually moved to Maui, following an impulse and, of course, a woman. It's hard to imagine now, but then we actually corresponded by mail, and so we cultivated an epistolary friendship. When a letter arrived to reveal that he had become a marijuana grower, I was intrigued but not surprised. It did seem like an appropriate enterprise for an athletic outlaw. His descriptions of Maui and his work served to prepare me for the abrupt transition that was to come.

After the last band disintegrated, I made my way to law school with the help of my father's connections but was an unenthusiastic student. Continual bickering with my longtime girlfriend contributed to my darkening depression. I confessed all this to William, and two weeks later a ticket to Maui arrived at my door. Included was a simple epigram, "Maui is the healer of all things human. Aloha, Will." And so I began my apprenticeship.

Christmas day that first year on Maui was memorable for its stunning beauty. I lived in a little room under the house and was awakened by the thumpings and excited exclamations of Stryder who was tearing open his presents even before first light. I waited a decent interval and then went upstairs to find William starting a fire in the wood stove and Laurie cooking pancakes with the contented, flushed look of someone who had recently experienced coitus.

We exchanged presents under a real Christmas tree from Oregon, and by nine o'clock we were at Baldwin Beach. The brilliant morning light turned the sand golden. There wasn't a cloud in the sky or a hint of wind. The West Maui mountains stood in sharp relief, every ridge and purple cleft revealed in utter clarity. The ocean, unusually calm, was turquoise near the shore, then lapis, azure, and, on the horizon, the deep cobalt of blue water. A fringe of white water appeared on the outer reef, the first evidence of a new swell. This was the tropical idyll I had always imagined.

Other families arrived including Jonas, his hippy wife and their three children. Presents were unwrapped, joints passes 'round. Aki also dropped by with Maile, his sister. She wore a single lei of tuber rose, the scent of which blended with the fragrance of the coconut oil she used as an emollient. Did I imagine the sweet aroma of her sex? Perhaps it was the tang of the ocean. She held herself apart but displayed no haughtiness, no conscious aloofness. Rather she seemed to be content with her own thoughts, comfortable in a private world. I was surprised, then, when she turned to me and asked if I was a writer. I told her that I had dabbled a bit in college but law school had consumed much of my time recently. "Perhaps you can help me sometime with my modest efforts," she said before unwrapping her pareu and diving into the water. I was elated but suppressed my emotions under the watchful eye of Aki. I suspected the hand of William in this, and I was right. He told me that night that he had extolled my literary accomplishments, which were actually limited to a few short stories in the Yale Lit. I would later be most grateful that he had burnished my reputation.

# CHAPTER V

THE NEXT DAY WILLIAM ANNOUNCED THAT IT was time to begin the new campaign, even though we were months away from planting anything. He wanted to take advantage of a spell of dry winter weather to begin moving fertilizer into the woods. First, though, he proposed that he and I reconnoiter an area that hadn't been worked in a couple of years. It was at a much higher elevation, over 3,500 feet, and had a climate and ecosystem that was much different than the lowlands. He explained that Green Harvest would certainly return to the scene of last year's rip off, so there was no point in going back there. "I want to re-familiarize myself with the area and see which spots still seem feasible. The trick is to have a patch that gets sufficient sunlight and yet is partially concealed by a few protruding tree limbs. Often we will climb up a tree and artfully lop off a few branches and then cover the exposed stumps with mud. Cutting down a whole tree would be a dead giveaway. A helicopter pilot once told me that a big patch is easy to see if you know where to look. The idea is not to give them cause to look at something in the first place. Really, patch placement is most essential to the art of pakalolo growing. And needless to say you have to find a rich vein of soil. But anyway our mission today will be fun. We won't carry any of the accouterments of growers. We will pretend to be hunting, and, who knows, maybe we will bag a pig."

"Pigs live up there too?"

"Yes, Sam." Will was patient. "Pigs live in the woods, as you recall, and some of the boars can be formidable at well over three hundred pounds with razor sharp tusks. And they are quick, too." My enthusiasm for the day hike was rapidly diminishing.

"How do we....'catch' one?"

"With this." He revealed a stainless steel Ruger .44 magnum revolver encased in a shoulder holster.

"Anyway we probably won't even see one, but we'll take Harry along, give him some exercise, and maybe he'll pick up a scent." Dirty Harry was the family pitbull who was especially protective of Stryder, never more than a few yards away from his little charge at any outdoor event. William called him the maitre d' because he carefully, and politely, took the measure of any visitor, never growling but never fawning, apprising one and all with a steady eye. He liked to chew on 2x4s.

After getting dropped off we set out through the emerald green pastures of the Haleakala Ranch, walking on a rough road that served the forest reserves. We crossed a cattle guard and passed through an improbable stand of eucalyptus trees, planted long ago in a mis-guided experiment. After a mile or so we left the road and headed down the mountain on a steep single track jeep trail. In less than an hour we emerged into a large grassy clearing and paused for a snack and a joint. Harry looked back and forth at the two of us until he got his expected biscuit. William explained that we would now head east into the native forest, an association of ohia and koa trees. We crossed one stream, then another, before ascending a steep hill-side. The entrance to the old patch was at the top of a small cliff which we scaled through a series of handholds composed of exposed tree roots. It was nearly vertical, and we had to push and pull Harry up the last ten yards or so. The patch was designed to be inaccessible to the "ground based rip-off" or hunter. Moreover, there was nothing to suggest a trail, and I complimented William on the clever-ness of the approach. He merely harumphed and said, "It will seem a lot less clever when you've got an eighty pound pack strapped on." I was already tired from the morning's exertions and couldn't imagine carrying a heavy load up the cliff.

Under the spreading branches of an ancient koa tree, the outlines of the old area were visible as well as the clearly demarcated terraces. I commented on the primitive farming techniques of a bygone culture. "Actually, Sam, the Hawaiians did cultivate in this general area. I've found irrigation ditches, stone walls, banana patches, wild taro, and even a tombstone. We can only speculate about the size of the pre-contact population." A gust of wind announced the arrival of a grey stream of clouds, turning the heat of the day suddenly cool. William pointed out that the wind was out of the south, which meant that a front was approaching, and we could expect rain in a day. This was the precursor to a "Kona storm," an advancing low pressure system out of the north that would draw moisture from the warmer southern latitudes. Heavy rain was often the result.

We were resting up against a tree when Harry quickly stood up, cocked his enormous head, and then lifted his muzzle as if to catch a scent. A few moments later he froze and stared intently upslope. We followed his gaze. A minute passed before we heard a distinct rustling in the underbrush above us. Instinctively William unholstered his revolver, and then suddenly a huge boar burst into our clearing. He lunged at Harry who deftly avoided his slashing tusks and with quick martial skill grabbed a hind leg. The enraged boar couldn't reach his adversary, and the determined pit was locked on, his eyes rolled back in his head. Around they went in a whirlwind, tumbling to the bottom of the patch, Harry unshakeable, unrelenting, never losing his grip on the pig's flesh. William waited until he had a clear shot; the explosion of the .44 could have been dynamite. The bullet entered through the left ear of the boar and blew out the right side of the his skull and the brain with it. The remaining half of the skull was absolutely clean, like the shell of an egg. Harry had to be coaxed into letting go, gradually relaxing as Will stroked his back, telling him what a good boy he was. My ears were ringing as William turned to me. "What a fucking mess!" I had thought he would be thrilled with our hunting prowess, but no. "There's no point in field dressing this beast. I'll just cut off the quarter sections and bury the rest. There are some old shovels hidden around here somewhere." He shook his head. "Laura will not be pleased. She's a vegetarian as you know, so I guess you and I will be roasting our dinner over a campfire in the backyard. And now we have a load to hump up the hill.... something spooked the pig, maybe hunters above us." He fell silent and then brightened. "On the other hand, we could invite the guys over for a barbeque and invest in a case of beer. We'll have a party!"

The cookout was a success; the tale of the hunt didn't even require hyperbole. Harry seemed to understand that he was the hero of the story, and he circulated among the guests, the recipient of much deserved adulation. David and Jonas were there of course, and W remarked favorably on the results of our scouting expedition. The grow sites still looked viable after a three year hiatus—no new trails hacked by hunters, tools well hidden, no evidence of other growers in the area. They all agreed that we should take advantage of the unusually benign winter weather and organize an early fertilizer run.

The next day we convened at the growers' store and filled the truck with bags of chicken shit, colloidal rock phosphate, greensand, kelp meal, potting soil, and assorted supplements.. We repaired to a warehouse in a former pineapple cannery that our crew had rented as a sort of command post. There we mixed the ingredients precisely, wearing respirators, and poured the blend into heavy duty plastic bags weighing eighty pounds each. We also prepared "Kokualani," the 1961

Willys 4x4 jeep truck that was used exclusively for supply runs. Powered by a super hurricane six engine and cooled by a Chevelle radiator with a fiberglass fan, she was the rugged embodiment of old school American manufacturing. The charging system was comprised of two batteries which powered a five ton Warn winch that housed fifty yards of cable. We tightened every bolt, changed all the fluids, and tuned the engine. A breakdown in the woods would be disastrous.

We decided to make our run with another crew, all friends, right around the January full moon. Dave had pals who worked for EMI, so we were able to borrow a key that worked for all the gates. Early in the evening we loaded Kokualani with forty 80 pound bags, over a ton and a half; the heavy duty leaf springs sagged a little. The other guys had an old International Harvester which carried a much lighter load.

At around 10 o'clock our little cohort started our drive from Haiku and on up Olinda Road to its terminus at Haleakala Ranch and the first gate. We were tense; William was driving of course.

There was little conversation, for we were vulnerable. Our intent was obvious, even though there was nothing illegal about driving around in the middle of the night with 3,000 lbs. of fertilizer. All was quiet as we approached the gate. It was a week night, and we had only encountered one car on the way up. David jumped out of the cab, found the right lock, opened it and waved us through. Jonas and I were riding in the back making sure the concealing tarp remained secure. Once through we turned off our head lights, easily making our way over the rough-hewn road by moonlight. Clouds raced overhead and I felt the occasional raindrop. After a couple of miles we reached the second gate, the beginning of the forest reserve. Towering cumulus clouds appeared in the eastern sky, and the wind freshened. The filtered lunar light gave the imposing trees a ghostly aspect.

The first squall hit us suddenly, a lashing rain that almost immediately penetrated my sweatshirt. William stopped the truck and dashed back to consult with the Harvester team. Dave said he couldn't guarantee the key again anytime soon; we would have to go for it, which meant turning off the relatively well-maintained EMI road and plunging down the steep jeep trail that W and I had hiked on our scouting trip. The rain did not abate, and as we made our way down the mountain, rivulets on the trail turned to streams; the dirt turned to slick mud. Our headlights were back on, but David used a handheld spotlight to penetrate the darkness ahead. The windshield wipers were useless. Will stuck his head out of the driver's window, steering with one hand. Jonas and I stood in the back, rocking and rolling like sailors on a storm-tossed ship, ducking to avoid low hanging branches. We finally arrived at the clearing that I recognized even in the darkness. We unloaded the vehicles quickly, carrying the bags to a depot fifty yards away. We would have to come back soon to more artfully hide everything.

The trip back up the mountain proved to be more challenging. Kokualani no longer had any weight over her rear axle, but in low range and first gear she tenaciously crept forward. The storm had intensified, and we heard the crack and rush of broken tree limbs above the howling wind. Rounding a sharp bend our passage was blocked by a fallen tree. Fortunately the other crew had a chainsaw, and they were able to cut out a section. We rolled it away and pressed on. The trail steepened and the Harvester had an increasingly difficult time before getting hopelessly stuck. We stopped our truck and went back to lend a hand and push; the spinning tires shot mud in our faces. The effect was comedic. Momentarily blinded we stumbled about like the drunken cast of a minstrel show. It was now about two o'clock in the morning, and only a few hours before dawn. We were cold, tired, muddy, and discouraged, but William had an inspiration. We would chain the Harvester to Kokualani and use the winch to pull both vehicles up the precipitous incline. It was impossible to shout above the roaring tempest, so we used flashlight signals. Two guys went ahead with the cable, fixing it to a tree. Three flashes of light meant that we could deploy the winch. W had admittedly never attempted such a load before, and a snapped cable under strain could have been deadly as well as leaving us stranded. With all in readiness he revved the engine, engaged the transmission, and hit the button on the winch control. Almost amazingly the train crept steadily forward. The cable had to be reset every hundred feet, so our progress was agonizingly slow. Eventually we were able to unchain the Harvester and proceed somewhat normally. Arriving back at the top, the moon was revealed again through scudding clouds.

We paused to crack open a six-pack and enjoy the slow ebb of adrenaline. We looked like abdominal wood creatures, eyes peering out of black face. Easy laughter seemed to dispel the last of the storm. We slipped out of the woods, just beating the gathering light. Hot showers, an omelet and deep sleep awaited us. We would make the run a couple of more times but under more auspicious circumstances. I took copious notes in my diary before submitting to a bone tired slumber.

# CHAPTER VI

THE STORM HAD TAKEN US BY SURPRISE, PERHAPS a foretaste of a wet spring. William said having the supplies in place was an important first step. We would now be able to hike the first several miles unencumbered before having to carry heavy packs. By February it was still too early to germinate, but we began the season by preparing the patches.

Our gang met with the Harvesters (we called them the Hardy Boys), and rode up all together to the top of Olinda Road in the back of our driver's pick-up truck. We hoped such a consolidation would minimize traffic and draw less attention to our project. Interestingly, the designated gathering place was the Yamamura farm. Papa-san was a hard working little Japanese man who rose every morning at three-thirty to begin his day. Will, a neighbor, had befriended him years earlier, and he heartily endorsed our work ethic and innovative approach to farming. That first day, as we discussed our agenda, Mama-san appeared, smiling, bearing mugs of hot coffee. She spoke almost no English, but William had coached her on growing a little backyard pakalolo patch of her own, eventually selling her produce and presenting her with a stack of hundred dollar bills. Mr. Y was head of the local Buddhist association, a respected member of the community, and actually fairly wealthy, although you never would have guessed it to look at him—a diminutive, sun-weathered figure in tattered overalls.

While Papa-san puttered about in the equipment shed, we smoked a joint and waited for Colleen, the driver. Sitting around a kerosene lantern, these gatherings offered us a chance to share some stories which I often recorded later in my notebook. David had to be coaxed into talking about his experiences in Viet Nam, but was often loquacious after a second cup of coffee. "Sure, humpin' an eighty pound pack is hard work, but ain't nobody trying to kill ya. My company was pinned down once for twenty-four hours, no food or water. Had some wounded, too, but it was too hot to risk a chopper. The fire fight lasted all night. It was the fuckin' Fourth of July! Muzzle flashes, tracer rounds, parachute flares, explosions, firecrackers—no, just kidding—noise that would mysteriously stop so that even the quiet seemed loud, if you can dig that. Some of the guys had dropped acid, and they thought it was beautiful, but I thought fuck that shit, I'll stick to reefer and keep my wits about me." To emphasize his point, David paused to take an extra big hit off the doobie. "By mid-morning we finally got air support. They dropped napalm. It was so close that I could feel the heat and shock wave rolling over the bunker. And that was that...." We quietly absorbed the idea of being burned alive by jellied gasoline while David stared at his boots and then resumed. "I hate war. All of it. I was just a dumb kid trying to live up to my Dad's expectations. And you know I came to admire the Cong—tough little fuckers." His story was interrupted by the sound of tires on gravel. Our driver had arrived, a bright hippy angel who elicited our grateful smiles and helped dispel the somber mood. David was aware that he had cast a pall over the group, so with deliberate cheerfulness he bellowed, "Let's pack it up. Time to hit the road."

I was always cold riding up the mountain in the back of a pick-up. It felt good to get out and start walking at a brisk pace. We tried to remain quiet, ever alert to another vehicle on the road, however unlikely in the dark pre-dawn. My most vivid memory is the richness of the night sky, the brightness of the stars, and the ascent of a neighboring planet, brighter still.

———

On the opening day of the new season, I was assigned my own patch to work. First we had to load our packs with the fertilizer that we had brought in several weeks before. With water, lunch, rain suit, gloves, and a hand saw, the packs weighed close to a hundred pounds. I could barely lift mine. I squatted so that William and Dave could wrestle it on to my back. I was instructed to pull all the straps snug, especially the hip belt so that the weight would be concentrated on the pelvic area. My first thought was that I was a victim of a cruel hazing, but even Jonas, the sinewy hippy, bore a similar burden with apparent ease. We had only marched a half a mile when we halted at my designated area. I realized then that the crew was being kind in assigning me the easiest patch. I was breathing hard, and my t-shirt was wringing wet although it was only 7:30 in the morning. "Well, Sam, have fun. Remember to dig the terraces really deep and thoroughly mix in the fertilizer. Look around for a shovel. There should be one from a couple of seasons ago. We'll be back by four or so."

"What if I get attacked by a boar?"

"Don't worry. That pig incident was quite rare."

"And the helicopters. What if….?"

"They don't fly at this time of year. You'll be fine." And with that they were gone.

I wiggled through a small tunnel in the stag horn, dragging my pack behind me. When I emerged in the clearing, I was wet, muddy, and chilled. We were working at an elevation of at least three thousand feet, and it was winter after all. Two weeks before Haleakala had been dusted with snow. I spread out a tarp to sit on and pulled on a sweatshirt. The sudden solitude was a little unnerving. I was alone in a forest, a wilderness, miles from civilization, on a strange island in the middle of the Pacific Ocean. I spent my first hour contemplating the play of light and shadow, listening to the wind in the trees, and deeply inhaling the oxygen rich mountain air. Soon the day was noticeably warmer, and I realized that I had better get to work. I found a shovel and began to turn the dirt over in the terraces. It was rich— black and loamy. William told me that the patch had been heavily fertilized in the past, and that he had added shredded hapu fern and decomposed tree bark to make the once clay-like soil drain better. Within ten minutes I was sweating again. I carefully added a double handful of fertilizer every three feet in each of the terraces, mixed it in, and marked each spot with a twig.

I had lunch in the shade and then took a nap. In the afternoon I finished my work and wondered again what future archeologists would think. I supposed that the tools would give us away as twentieth century farmers, albeit primitive ones. I had been intrigued by W's discovery of abandoned homesteads and attempted to do a little research at the local library. I wasn't able to discover much but found that the forest was an important resource for the Hawaiians. Indeed, the name of our little hometown, Makawao, means "edge of the forest." Poʻokela Church, a substantial structure, sits just above town and was founded by missionaries in 1843. Plainly they recognized the importance of the area, perhaps as a spiritual nexus for the indigenous population. Did the natives flee to the woods to escape the devastating effects of white man's diseases? Or were they there all along? Certainly there was an abundance of water while only a few miles away in Kula there was none. Little information is contained in the historical record.

A sudden rustling in the brush snapped me out of my reverie, but it was only William coming through the tunnel. I hadn't spoken a word in eight hours, although I had taken plenty of notes in my journal. Will gazed admiringly at my work. "Well, Sam, you did an excellent job. I can envision eight foot plants bristling with buds." As usual I felt a trill of pride at William's praise. I felt comfortable in the role of little brother, perhaps because I never had a sibling of my own. And yet there was something ludicrous about two Yale graduates conferring about a piece of dirt in the middle of the wilderness. I expressed as much to William. "Oh, Sam. It's part of the process. An essential part. Without good soil you can't have good plants. And look at this place, how it catches the sun, the long western exposure with a commanding view of the West Maui Mountains, all artfully obscured by a few branches. It is elegant, fraught with possibility. It expresses a certain aesthetic that you will come to appreciate."

We joined the others and after a smoke break headed down the mountain rather than walking back up. It was easy going, and we tripped along at a good pace, ultimately descending about 1,500 vertical feet, following pig trails for the most part. I learned how to gently brush vegetation aside rather than breaking it, and how to carefully step on solid ground rather than in the mud in order to minimize our tracks. For my partners it was an unconscious, graceful dance. Indeed it was a pleasure to move so freely without the weight of a heavy pack. We crossed the formidable Opana Gulch and ended up in rolling green pasture land. A little after dark Colleen appeared at the pick up spot and handed each of us a cold beer and an 800 mg ibuprofen. The next day I was so sore and tired that I could barely get out of bed. It amazes me still that we worked fifteen hour days. Even though we only did this two or three days a week, I remember being exhausted much of the time. Gradually my strength and stamina increased, and I felt physically powerful in a way that I never had before. Most days were like the first, with subtle variations, but one day stood out in particular.

By April spring time rains were the norm, but one morning a heavy rain began shortly before dawn and never let up. We spent much of our time huddled under a tarp, hoping for a break in the weather; work was impossible. In mid-afternoon the rain intensified, becoming torrential. Veins of coursing water began to form around us. William jumped up. "We have to get out of here. The ground is already saturated. The streams can come up quickly and it might have been raining even harder up the mountain." We folded up the tarp and were quickly soaked; our expensive gortex rain suits were useless against the deluge. We headed down the mountain, tacking west.

The first small stream we came to, which normally gurgled enthusiastically, was raging at its banks and rising by the second. We linked arms and crossed at a wide point where the water was slightly less turbulent. Hurrying, our little platoon forded another stream successfully and then, coming to Opana Gulch, stopped in amazement. The Gulch is a prominent geological feature of East Maui, a very deep and narrow ravine that drains a large part of the watershed. It was, that evening, like nothing the lads had ever seen. Conversation was difficult above the incessant roar of white water. Huge tree trunks were tossed about like matchsticks; massive booming boulders bounced downstream like marbles. We were trapped. There was nothing to do but set up the tarp, smoke a joint, eat the last of our food, and settle in for a long wait.

By eleven o'clock the rain had stopped, and a waning moon appeared through broken clouds. The water began to drop noticeably, although it was still inconceivably dangerous. A cold wind swept down the mountain and chilled us to the bone. Someone had a small transistor radio and dialed in a rock station from Oahu. We danced around crazily to keep warm. A couple of hours later the water had receded considerably, to the point where we could attempt a crossing. Cautiously we edged into the torrent, searching for the safest route by the light of the moon. I was last in line, carefully watching Jonas ahead of me, when I slipped and was immediately swept downstream. I hadn't gone more than twenty yards when I struck a concrete weir or dam. The force of the water pressed me hard against it, face first, which was good because I could inch my way along to the opposite bank. My head created a small air pocket so that I could breathe. The guys quickly formed a chain, anchored by a rope around Dave's waist, and I felt William's firm grasp on my forearm, pulling me to safety. As I lay on the ground gasping, I could hear Jonas offering a prayer. William was shaken. "We almost lost you Samuel. If you had gone over the weir....well...."

"But you were cool, dude." It was Dave. "Kept your head. Did what you had to." He slapped me on the back. "Love you man. Now let's get the fuck out of here."

Of course the ride was long gone, and this was way before the era of the cell phone. We had no choice but to keep walking to Makawao. We arrived in town about two in the morning. The local hot spot, Piero's Bar and Disco, was still going strong. After a short conference an emissary was dispatched into the club to negotiate a ride. Fortunately, Opana had scoured us clean, although our clothes were completely soaked. While the rest of us hid behind the building, Dave, a single man, went in eagerly, perhaps hoping for a last call assignation. He emerged instead with Bob, a thoroughly drunk fellow grower who naturally sympathized with our plight. We got our ride and confronted a distraught Laurie who rustled up a

big meal, drew hot baths, and allowed us to sleep
past noon.

It was after this incident that I began to seriously
question my involvement in the marijuana growing
business. What at first seemed like a lark now
seemed like brutally hard work with potentially
fatal consequences. I expressed my misgivings to
William and asked exactly how much we could
expect to gain from our adventure. "Well, Samuel,
I don't want you to labor under a false impression.
You saw what happened last year. We probably
could have made more working as waiters in
Ka'anapali, god forbid. We have to contend with
rip-offs, Green Harvest, natural disasters, crit-
ters—rats, pigs, wild cattle—I could go on. But
ok, the upside is several hundred thousand dollars. You have to expect to lose a good percentage.
It is risky, no doubt. Storing it, transporting it,
selling it, carrying the money—risky too." I was
somewhat mollified by the prospect of a big pay
day, but we were hardly in the same league as
cocaine smugglers. "Fuck cocaine, Sam. I mean I
like to party in the city, but it's a business founded
on death and addiction. We aren't drug dealers;
we're farmers, herbalists, naturalists, outdoorsmen,

hunters. We bring joy to people, Sam. We keep our karma clean. I've never sold a dime's worth of coke and I never will. I know growers who invested their money in it and look at them now. Fat drug addicts who are bringing the heat on the rest of us." I mentioned his involvement with Madeline and wondered if that posed something of a contradiction. "I grant your point. It is true that I look the other way with certain people whom I regard as friends. All I can say is that I won't sell it. That's the best that I can do. At least Madeline doesn't step on it."

I thanked Will for the pep talk and thought how nice it would be to have some money. I could go back to law school without having to ask my parsimonious father for a cent and perhaps buy a nice car, unlike my current five hundred dollar piece-of-shit "Maui cruiser" with a hole in its muffler. "Samuel, haven't I always had your best interests at heart?" He threw an arm around my shoulder. "You certainly remember the mescaline business back in college? Of course you do! You made out pretty well if I recall. You were able to attract the attention of some pretty hot girls— women, whatever—and it's not like you had much else going for you." I just had to laugh, caught up again in William's infectious exuberance and the remembrance of our undergraduate days. Our conversation was interrupted when Laura entered the room with a wry grin.

"Ok you two. Samuel, do you know something about my husband that I don't?" I was embarrassed, but my laughter was intractable. "Give it up, Sammy!" she declared, hands on hips. Stryder zoomed by and rammed his Hot Wheels into the refrigerator. I looked at Will who gave me silent permission with a sly smile and a shrug.

"Ok. ok." I gathered myself. "William's pals from high school were chemistry majors at Berkeley. They made the best synthetic mescaline on the West Coast. We would fly out there and bring back the concentrate, a very small amount of which would buff out to a thousand hits using dicalcium phosphate. The stuff was potent, and the measurements had to be so exact that the only place with the necessary equipment was the Kline Biology Tower which had sophisticated state-of-the-art electronic scales. We would dress up in white lab coats, shoo away the graduate students—pretending that we had permission from some eminence—and, after locking the doors, quickly do our work. Voila! Pounds of the best mescaline anywhere." I looked over at Laura to gauge the effect of my story. Her expression was one of controlled neutrality. William sat down at the kitchen table and continued.

"Perhaps we were a little cheeky. Anyway, Darling, it was pretty lucrative. We had to cap the stuff wearing gloves and masks, and the 'capping parties' became notorious. Everyone got high inadvertently." Laura crossed her arms and shook her head.

"So that's what an Ivy League education is good for? What a couple of jokers. Do you know how hard I had to work to put myself through San Diego State?"

"Come, come. Working as an exotic dancer couldn't have been that hard." I felt that William had crossed a line and was skating on thin ice, mixed metaphors be damned. She shot him daggers. "Now Honey," said W, becoming unctuous, "we were semi-serious students. Hell, Sam eventually got into law school, admittedly years later, but nonetheless…. Oh could you fix us a couple of omelets; we're starving." She looked at him in amazement.

"Fuck you, William. Fix them yourself! You two are a couple of home-ec majors." After she marched out of the kitchen, Will opened a couple of beers and we toasted our friendship while Stryder dug into a carton of chocolate ice-cream. The omelets we made were delicious.

# CHAPTER VII

With the moon nearly full in April, it was time to germinate our seeds. Jonas consulted an astrological chart for the most propitious day. All we had to carry was much lighter potting soil which we used to fill small plastic cups. In each bag William placed a carefully chosen seed—fat and hard with "tiger stripes," a hallmark of his carefully cultivated strain. The bags were placed in a wire mesh cage to protect them from birds and rodents. Will explained that the original "Maui Wowie" paka-lolo was a result of crossing Thai Golden Voice, an effervescent, cerebral sativa, with an Afghani hash plant which gave our pot a "bass note, a bottom, like a kick drum." Every year the guys grew a small seed patch, selecting the earliest declaring male to pollinate the best looking lady plants, resulting in a bias toward early harvest. I compared W favorably to Gregor Mendel. "Yes, Sam it's true. This is where the art and science of pot growing meet. This vial of seeds is as important to us as any aspect of our endeavor. We have a genetic code like nobody else. Our pot is superior to anything on the market, and that's why our customers pay top dollar." He wired the cage tight and we lifted it on to an elevated platform made of tree branches. "Now we just need a light, steady spring rain." Almost immediately clouds streamed in from the east, and small drops began gently falling. "The gods are with us." William held his hands together in supplication and looked upward. "Hopefully we will be able to put these seedlings in the ground in about three weeks." He was silent for a minute and then became pensive. "We need a good year, Sam. The house is unfinished, as you know, and of course poverty puts a strain on any relationship. Stryder has to go to pre-school in the fall. The truck needs serious work, etc. To be a grower is ignominious enough, but to be a failed grower is embarrassing. You've wasted a year and can't get back in the saddle until the next seasonal cycle. Laurie is understanding, but if we don't pull it off this year, well, I might have to get a job." He said this in a funereal tone, as if it were a jail sentence.

I pointed out that many people had jobs and even found a measure of satisfaction in their work, and that, further, they didn't run the risk of incarceration or cruel death. This did little to dispel Will's sudden gloom. "Sam, I cannot have some asshole telling me what to do and when to do it." I suggested that something entrepreneurial might serve, something, heaven forbid, legitimate. "Yeah, maybe." He stroked his beard, turning over that thought. "The truth is I just love growing pot. I am Taoist. I like being tuned in to the rhythms and cycles of nature. I like weather. I like sunshine. I like rain. I like to hike. I like a whiff of danger. I like silence. I like to nap under a tree. The New York thing is what I have to do, and I try to make it fun, but this is what I really like to do. It is my metier. Anyway," he said more cheerfully, "let's go meet the guys and see how they fared." The drizzle had become constant, and we found Dave and Jonas sitting under a tarp, predictably smoking a joint. Jonas' long, wet hair was matted to his face which was streaked with mud.

"Tonto here did a face plant," said Dave, carefully blowing smoke rings through a smile. "But we did germinate the Garden of Eden, the Galaxy, and the Big Apple, not withstanding. God this reminds me of Nam, the good part of it anyway. I know I harp on it…. sorry."

"No, David," said Jonas thoughtfully. "It's good for you to share these things. How else are you going to come to grip with your demons? I've heard that killing people causes more stress than being killed, or something like that."

Dave gave him a sideways glance. "Jesus, Jonas, you are so stoned. Fuck, I don't know if I killed anybody. I might have, but it wasn't like Davey Crocket at the Alamo. I mean mostly we were just shooting at muzzle flashes and flickering shapes in the jungle. But people were killed and worse, horribly wounded. Some guys made out pretty well though, smuggling drugs. Body bags full of smack, Saigon to Travis AFB. The CIA helped them out, too, in order to finance the warlords up north. Funny thing is, even the Cong got involved. Of course, they didn't call themselves that, but everybody knew. And what better way to attack America than to bomb New York with kilos of heroin?"

Jonas was puzzled. "But David, how did you know all this? Weren't you what was called, no offense, a grunt?"

"Me? Oh I accidentally discovered a group working out of the PX one night when I was trying to steal some liquor. One of the guys was a buddy. They brought me in, put me on the payroll as a consultant and let me know that a general was involved by way of telling me to keep my trap shut. And that's how I was able to buy a little piece of this rock when I was discharged." We digested this bit of information, finished the joint, zipped up our raincoats, took down the tarp, and headed down the mountain.

# CHAPTER VIII

THE GERMINATIONS WERE STAGGERED SO THAT we could process our harvest in increments. The next favorable day was a week away so we had a little time off. I was surprised to get a phone call from Maile who wanted me to critique the first several chapters of her novel which was set during the overthrow of Hawaii's last monarch, Queen Lili'uokalani. We agreed to meet at the east end of Baldwin Beach under the shade of the ironwood trees. She thoughtfully brought a picnic lunch which included a chilled bottle of Riesling. "I included the wine only to pair with our snack, not to favorably influence your criticism." She said this with a smile. "Besides my professors at Stanford were demanding, so I can take a little heat." We settled on a blanket and uncorked the bottle. "So here it is, the first four chapters anyway." She handed me a typed manuscript, double spaced, which I accepted reverentially and began to read. After a few pages I realized that she had an extraordinary gift. Her description of old Honolulu perfectly evoked the time and place with simple, un-embroidered lyricism. I eagerly read on, and when I paused for a sip of wine, I found her gazing intently at me, her large brown eyes searching mine. "Well?"

"You write very well," was all I managed to say, for in that moment I was freshly smitten. I had acknowledged her beauty months ago, but now I was stuck by her brilliance, her depth. I had to upbraid myself for having dismissed her earlier as just another beach ornament, albeit a very fetching one. She leaned in close and pointed a long finger at a paragraph on page twelve. "Is this perhaps too didactic?" I inhaled her scent while she waited for a reply, but I was fascinated by the outline of her mons veneris which thrust against her bikini bottom. "Come on, Sam. I asked you a question." Her earnestness snapped me out of my reverie. I mumbled a reply which must have been satisfactory since she broke into a big smile. "I didn't think so either! I need to dramatize the plight of my people." Her dimples emphasized a set of radiantly white teeth, offset by flawless brown skin. Until that moment I had never thought of her in ethnic terms; her beauty seemed instead to place her in another, transcendent realm. So she was a political creature as well. How could a Stanford grad be otherwise?

After reading the manuscript we went swimming before lunch. She knotted her long black hair in a bun and slipped into the water, swimming with an efficient grace, hardly leaving a wake. I struggled to keep up but was motivated by the sight of her tight buttocks swiveling in perfect rhythm. Back on the beach I commented on her exquisite form. "Well, I trained for years. I went to Stanford on an athletic scholarship." After lunch we finished the wine, and Maile lay on her back, stretched out on a towel. She closed her eyes and must have known that I was carefully regarding her long limbs, trim tummy, and pert little breasts. She opened an eye. "Thanks for your help. I'll keep you in mind when choosing an editor. I like you, Samuel." She laughed. "You're ok for a haole."

When I got home I confided to Laurie that I was falling for Maile and asked her forthrightly what she thought my chances were. She considered her response longer than I had hoped. "Well, you are both smart and educated, but she is only in her twenties. No big deal I guess, but there are, well, cultural differences. There might be some family objections since you are, as you know, a mainland haole. If you are just looking to get laid, there are plenty of hussies in Lahaina. Try the Blue Max on Friday night." I must have blushed. Hearing the beautiful Laura talk about sex made me uncomfortable. I replied that my feelings were somewhat deeper. "Ok. You just need to know that she is the pride and joy of a large, extended local family." When I mentioned this conversation to William he was surprisingly thoughtful.

"I don't know, Sam. You need to be clear in your intentions. We are a very closed society here. Of course that is changing everyday as more and more people invade our little island. There is a degree of acceptance that didn't exist ten years ago. Still, you would be under close scrutiny, and you wouldn't want to run afoul of her people, trust me. Personally, I would look elsewhere. This windsurfing craze is attracting some amazing women. Man, if I weren't married I would run amok." His thoughts now turned elsewhere, but I was thankful for his insights. We decided to learn to windsurf, but I couldn't get Maile out of my mind. That night I took copious notes in my dairy and was reminded of Jorge Luis Borges' cautionary quip, "To fall in love is to create a religion that has a fallible god."

# CHAPTER IX

AS SPRING PROGRESSED AND THE DAYS LENGTH-ened, the weather began to dry up. The rain line had retreated eastward and we followed it, germinating the last patches in May. The final area was at the extreme limits of our domain. Indeed it was in the heart of the wilder-ness, and we had to camp overnight at a site the guys had prepared years before. Their equipment had been stashed in waterproof bags and well hidden. There was a tent (a bit mildewy), sleeping bags, cooking utensils, and a propane camp stove. We set up the tent on flat mossy ground that overlooked a small waterfall. Dinner consisted of crackers, cheese, a couple of apples, and a small bottle of tequila. The next morning Jonas sur-prised us with pancake batter and jug of maple syrup. Fortunately the stove still worked. I had to marvel at having buckwheat cakes and hot coffee in the middle of nowhere.

On the second day, with our now familiar work completed, our eremitic little band began the long march westward down and across the mountain. Harry accompanied us on this expedition because we knew that he had the uncanny ability to pick out the right trail, while the collective human memory was apt to be a little hazy.

The heavy rains of April had moderated considerably. Now we usually experienced early morning showers which cleared after an hour or two. By the end of May the seeds we had germinated in April had transmogrified into sturdy seedlings, fairly bursting out of their cages. It was springtime. The forest, the earth itself, was in a state of lusty verdure. The sun had a markedly greater intensity, and the first heat of the day lifted steam from the rich soil, quickly drying the surrounding vegetation. It was t-shirt weather at last. William said that conditions were absolutely perfect.

Each seedling was carefully planted, and we often stood back and admired our handiwork, each of us offering a silent benediction. I often thought about what success would mean for me. I could return to law school on my own terms, perhaps with a measure of style. I was older than most of my fellow students, and the idea of working in some poorly paid university job was anathema to me. Then, too, I often wondered if I even gave a shit about law school. Really, perhaps more than anything, I wanted to impress Maile. I could take her to New York, hire a carriage for a ride through Central Park, hear jazz in the Village, take in a Broadway play, stay in the Plaza and make love high above the distant throb and pulse of the city. So far, we had only gone out on a single date, a safe enough outing to the local movie theater to see a film that we both hated. In my poverty I took refuge in my daydreams.

For my "big brother" William, I knew that a good year would mean a renewal of family life. The successful hunter would be feted by his little tribe, and his esteem would rise in the eyes of his warrior queen whom he truly loved. W embraced the contradictions that most, if not all, men did. His dedication to his family was in no way mitigated by a roving eye or the occasional indiscretion. The latter he always justified in anthropological terms, an elaborate rationalization for dangerous liaisons.

David was a simpler man, a community college drop out who nevertheless had a fierce intelligence and a remarkably compassionate side. He liked to tease William about married life, living with "a ball and chain" and all that, but he clearly had a real affection for Laura and little Stryder. He even admitted to a certain amount of envy, especially when he was invited to dinner. He never left without a good rough house with Stryder who adored "Uncle Davey." I think he was just wisely waiting for the right girl.

Jonas was also a family man whose wife, Sunshine, was pure hippy gothic. In the 1980s she seemed like a throwback to an earlier time, that is to say the nineteen sixties. Radiant, beatific, and pretty in a plain way, Sunny devoted herself to a growing brood of urchins which often included the neighborhood kids. She ran a wonderful little pre-school, "fully licensed" she was proud to say, which catered largely to pot growers. Jonas envisioned this as the beginning of a "spiritual center" which he would someday build on his land in Huelo. The New Age movement was thankfully not yet a presence on Maui, so clearly Jonas was ahead of his time, a prescient visionary.

Once all the "starts" were planted we really did have a break. William said the keikis would grow quite well on their own and that visiting them unnecessarily would only leave more pronounced trails. In mid-summer we would have to begin tending the patches religiously, once a week, in order to cut out the male plants which declared their sex earlier than the females. In the meantime we were to enjoy a hiatus, a deserved break from the rigors of the spring. Unfortunately we were just about broke, and rather than having a real vacation we were forced to confront the dire reality of our situation. Laura gamely took a part-time job hostessing at a fancy restaurant in Wailea which was helpful but only put more pressure on the purported bread winners to do something, anything.

At this critical juncture William received a fortuitous phone call from George, the Old Poet, a former professor of ours who now taught at the University of Hawaii. He had a proposition for us, but was somewhat cagey over the phone. Will had kept in touch over the years, supplying George and his academic cohort with pot, a small retail business that allowed him to surf on Oahu. We were to come to Honolulu, bringing the usual purchase, and The Poet would reveal his plan to us. There was an unspoken cloak and dagger aspect to this which immediately appealed to William.

The "Old Poet" was an appellation that we had conferred upon George at Yale, although he was then only in his fifties. He taught a course in Eastern Mystical Poetry and enjoyed reading his own translations of erotic poetry to a decidedly coed class of young men and women. He was reasonably fluent in Japanese, Korean, and "gook" (as he put it), a result of his Naval Intelligence training. His academic credentials merely enhanced his deeper military immersion. He had great stories about his involvement with the CIA which he divulged only when he was fairly inebriated. As undergraduates William and I encouraged him in this and often spent drunken evenings in his New Haven apartment being regaled by tales of derring do and utter ineptitude.

W and I got As in his course because we supplied him with pot, but it wasn't marijuana that led to George's downfall. A sexual harassment suit was brought against him by the infamous Mindy "Catscratch" Lydgate, a cheerleader and a niece of one of the trustees. She alleged the Professor agreed to a bout of fellatio in exchange for a coveted A that would lift her g.p.a. out of marginal danger. George put up a spirited defense, insisting that the sexual act was consensual and was, in fact, an example of "soix ante neuf." But Mindy was too good. According to The Poet she pointed her finger at him and, with perfect timing, broke into tears. Her many notorious campus assignations were somehow not deemed admissible evidence against her now sullied reputation. CIA/Yale connections were called, and it was arranged for George to take a position at the University of Hawaii in faraway Honolulu. He had to sign an oath to never again set foot on the Yale campus. A few trustees intimated that the punishment would be grave indeed. As for Mindy, the generous settlement with the university meant that she could ditch her rich boyfriend and pursue the life of an expatriate hedonist. Even George frankly admired the way she had gamed the system. "Damn it," he used to say, "she really did deserve an A."

—

It was easy to find George. He occupied the same booth every Friday afternoon in his favorite bar. It was an old-fashioned place on King Street that smelled of disinfectant and stale beer. Dark and cavernous, it afforded a pleasant contrast to the blinding glare and noise of the street, although the slowly revolving ceiling fan did little to stir the fetid air. "You assholes are late as usual!" The Old Poet's saturnine countenance became visible in the gloom. He was working on a beer, a chaser for the several shots of tequila that he had already downed. The empty shot glasses were lined up neatly. I hadn't seen George in years; W warned me that he could be grumpy, but that he would actually be glad to see us. "Well, Bingham," he addressed me as he had in college, "you're looking fit. How could it be otherwise, hanging out with Romeo here." He signaled Mabel, the old Japanese waitress, to bring us a couple of beers. Frowning, she did his bidding. "That's a good girl, darling," George said when she returned. He gave her a pinch on the butt which, strangely, elicited a giggle. Plainly he was a regular and a good tipper.

("You a naughty boy, Mr. G.") We did the pot deal in plain sight, and The Poet couldn't suppress a smile. "Ok, now you have the money, so the next round's on you."

We knew George would divulge his proposal in good time, so we ordered pu-pus and more beer. A cheap looking Korean woman, almost ghoulish in her heavy make up and clad only in a red chemise, appeared out of nowhere and slid in next to The Poet. "You buy me champagne?" she cooed.

"Not now, Michelle. I'm taking care of business." She pouted and left our presence. "Reminds me of Subic Bay, boys. Or Saigon. That's why I love this place."

William spoke up. "Well Professor, you are still an incorrigible rake." William had always loved to needle George, especially regarding his sexual misadventures. "As part of your settlement with Yale didn't you have to go to counseling?" I thought this intentional goad might provoke The Poet, but instead he just grinned.

"Well, fuck you very much, it worked out just fine. You see, Ms. Taylor, the psych doctor, was a real looker. And she used her charms to bewitch her patients, at least me. Her professional skirt was way too short to begin with, and when she sat down she made no attempt to keep it from riding up. Oh, she was wiley that Dr. Taylor! Crazy smart too—Columbia med—and of course she knew that she was driving me wild. I honestly thought that it was part of a therapy since I was supposed to be a sex maniac or something. Was I to learn restraint? Maybe I really did suffer from acute satyriasis. Then, too, her questions about my sexual procliv-ities were rather pointed. Finally I could take it no longer. I felt that I was coming to the intended climax of the therapy. Without thinking the ques-tion simply erupted from me. 'Are we going to have sex?' 'I thought you'd never ask,' replied she, rising and unbuttoning her blouse. And so we did! On her Freud style couch, she straddling me."

"Did you have more sessions?" Now George had us; we weren't smirking anymore.

"Hell yes! Somebody was paying for it—Yale, the union, I don't know." The thought of someone else paying for "it" struck us dumb for a minute. "You see boys, that's why I'm Herr Professor and you are my humble students."

"Touché, Herr Professor." We held up our glasses in salute. "That was a masterful stroke." He returned the acknowledgement with a raised shot glass.

Relaxed now in his oneupmanship, George ordered another beer and started to outline his proposal. Prolix as always he began by narrating a back story. As we knew, he lived in downtown Honolulu (before it was fashionable) and was a widely recognized figure in that small world. He reminded us that as the unofficial mayor he took a broad interest in the welfare of local residents, often stopping to help a senior cross the street or carry her groceries. One day, as the story went, he held up traffic to aid an elderly, slightly confused Japanese gentleman in his attempt to cross Bethel Street against the light. The two men ran into each other often after that and became regular breakfast companions at Irma's, famous for its crab omelets. The owlish and unprepossessing Mr. Mirikitani was, as it turned out, the former, but long retired, head of a local crime syndicate whose primary interest was gambling, although they had their fingers in many pies, some of them semi-legitimate. Operations had been turned over to his oldest son for some time. When "Boy" eventually met George, he thanked him for his kindness to the old man, and The Poet became the beneficiary of considerable largess. A two year old Coupe de Ville was among the many things that Boy discarded and passed on. It was parked outside the bar.

Recently Mr. M confided to George that he needed help with a problem. A dispute had arisen within the Suzuki family fish business. An elder brother was attempting to steal the business from his two sisters, Phyllis and Gladys, and was strong-arming local fishermen into working only with him. The two women had control of the processing facility but were unable to get any fish. Mr. M would have ordinarily used his influence to help them, but some inscrutable code prevented him from intervening in an intra-family dispute. He made it clear, though, that his sympathies were entirely with the sisters. Did George know of someone, from Maui perhaps, who could come to the aid of the desperate damsels? "And that's where you ne'r-do-wells come in." Addressing William he continued. "You grew up in this god-forsaken archipelago. With all your connections you must know some fishermen." Will replied that he did indeed, and in fact one was a boyhood friend who worked out of the Big Island. "If you can get fish to Honolulu, there's money to be made....for all of us." The Poet leaned back, arms crossed, and then slowly smiled at William's enthusiastic response. "You guys can spend the night in my loft, and I'll take you to meet the sisters in the morning."

"But first we have to go to a poetry reading. You heard me. There is some dipshit from New York who is visiting on a fellowship. He's giving a reading tonight at the Crossroads coffee house. I'm his minder. Why do you think I'm drinking so heavily? He wears a man-purse for chrissake! The women love him, though, and I can guarantee some intellectual ass will be there. Right up your alley, right?" He paused to leer. "If you two can act mopey, vulnerable, or better yet, needy, you might get laid out of the situation. C'mon boys!

Let's take a ride in my Cadillac." He tossed the waitress a hundred dollar bill and we were off.

—

George was required to bring the refreshments, so after a mandatory stop at the liquor store we arrived at the poetry venue well in advance of the anticipated crowd. "It's a wine and cheese affair, Jesus help me. I'll put this rot-gut out for the masses and stow a couple of good bottles for us. Now I have to go and fetch the Great Man. Why don't you make yourselves useful and put out some chairs. And be on your best behavior." It was early evening on a warm summer night when the audience began to trickle in. Many were older academics, but there were more than a few earnest grad school women dressed flamboyantly, and a smattering of hipsters, attracted no doubt by the promise of free booze. A small stage had been set up for His Eminence, as George called him. George was supposed to handle the introduction, but as the start time approached he was nowhere to be seen. We finally found him backstage sitting against a wall, a nearly empty wine bottle at his side. His white beard was stained purple from the grape; a dopey, vinolent grin spread across his mug. "Ok. I know what you're thinking. The Professor is a little drunk. 'Tis true, 'tis true. Damn, that was a choice year for Burgundy! So now one of you is going to have to introduce this fatuous clochard. Here's his bio....got it somewhere.... hmm." He produced a crumpled piece of paper from his vest pocket. "Say I'm indisposed, whatever. I'll try to sober up in time to hit on some of the lovelies." With that he fell over and began to snore loudly.

It was then that William "volunteered" me. "A perfect role for you Samuel. You're the son of a preacher man. You can affect the necessary senorous tone. I remember you doing Shakespeare in college." He glanced at George. "I'm just glad he passed out now and not onstage." I readily agreed, being a little tipsy myself, and went to greet the Eminence who was preening in the wings. He looked me up and down, sniffed once, and offered a limp, fishy hand. I explained that the Professor had suffered a seizure and would need a couple of hours to recover. Without waiting for a response, I went to the lectern and began my spiel. I thanked all the various foundations, the NEA, and the university for funding the fellowship and praised the Great Man's poetry effusively. Only a few of the brighter lights picked up on my sardonic edge. In fact I couldn't stand the man's writing. Much to his annoyance I chose to remain seated on the stage, much like an effete play-goer in a Restoration comedy, purposely stealing attention. From my vantage point I could look out at the audience, slowly scanning the crowd for the hottest women. It was the only way to stay awake, an antidote to the dolorous rumblings of the GM. Then suddenly I was shocked into wakefulness. My heart raced. I stared hard to be sure, but there was no mistake. It was Maile in the back row. When I recovered somewhat I took note of the fact that she was sitting next to a blonde fellow with John Lennon glasses. Were they holding hands? It was hard to see. The next hour passed quickly. Soon it was time for the book signing (a very slim volume) and the proffered wine. I was wondering how to engage Maile when she appeared in front of me.

"Sam, I had no idea you knew....(here she named our guest poet). You've been holding out on me Samuel! I had no idea that you hung out in such exalted literary circles. And to think, you're my editor! Oh my god." Richard, her date, hung back before being properly introduced. "Let's get a glass of wine." She grabbed me by the arm and quickly led me away. "I'm here to apply to the PhD. program, and Richard is a....friend. Sam, look me up back on Maui. Please." William appeared with exquisite timing and threw an arm around my shoulder.

"Well, Mai, fancy seeing you here. Didn't I tell you that our man Sam is a widely recognized man of letters?" I hoped that he wouldn't lay it on too thick, but he backed off. "I know you two would love to chat, but we have to deal with the Professor."

The hard part was wrestling George into the Caddy since he was a large man and unsteady on his feet. Lying down in the back seat, he barked out instructions, and we successfully navigated our way to his Soho style loft in an old warehouse. Surprisingly, he was the first one up in the morning, bright eyed and bushy tailed. With a chef's apron covering his ample bulk and waving a spatula as he cooked, he announced breakfast. "Coffee's on and I'm scrambling some eggs with a side of bacon. Toast's up and the jam is on the table." Steaming mugs in hand, we reviewed the events of the previous evening. "Well, nobody got lucky, and that's the bad news. On the other hand I'm rid of what's-his-name. He's staying with somebody in the English department." I mentioned that although I hadn't gotten lucky in the conventional sense, I did have the good fortune to make a favorable impression on the beauteous Maile, my beau ideal. I admitted to being a little perturbed by her reference to her "friend." I queried my companions as to the possible meaning. "Well," said the Professor, "I have been a life-long student of muliebrity, and it can only mean one of two things. Either she's fucking him or she isn't. Intentionally ambiguous, I'd say, but that's women for you. I will say that gals often use the term 'special friend' to indicate a sexual relationship....if that makes you feel any better."

After breakfast we made our way to the sisters' facility down by the commercial piers in Honolulu Harbor. George, now the perfect gentleman, introduced us. We liked the soft-spoken, alert women immediately, although it was hard to tell them apart since they both had tight grey perms and wore identical square rimmed glasses and creased polyester pants. We agreed to fly to the Big Island and get in touch with William's fishermen friends in Hilo.

The next day a conference was called at the Hilo Bay Hotel. Just before dawn the fishermen trooped in—hearty lads, unshaven, smelling of fish scales and blood, cigarette smoke and booze. Black coffee was served, laced with whiskey, and someone passed a joint around. Jeb, their out-sized leader, offered William a calloused paw and a big grin. "Nice to see you again, bro'." The crew was a bunch of hard working haoles who divided their time between fishing and pot growing, and they were only moderately successful in both endeavors. Will surmised that they were tired of being ripped off by the wholesaler at Hilo Bay and was sure that we could get them a better price from the Suzuki sisters if only we could get the ahi to Honolulu. He explained the situation and potential difficulties to Jeb. We would pay cash, handle the shipping, and get paid in turn by the sisters who needed product right away to stay in business. Jeb didn't think for long before replying. "Well, we're down to it. Harvest is months away, and the price of fuel ain't gettin' any cheaper. What do say, boys? You know the goons'll try to lean on us if we don't sell to them, but I say to hell with those assholes." He looked around at the grizzled band who eagerly voiced their assent. "Ok bro', we're in. But you gotta know that they're gonna come after you too." William was resolute.

"Yeah, I know, but we're not without friends of our own."

"Well, you're gonna need 'em." There was a solemn pause. Jeb was an old friend of Will, and I knew that he was concerned. "Alright, then. We'll see you tomorrow with our catch." I, too, had put on a brave face, but I was beginning to wonder exactly what we were getting into.

The following day we took delivery of two giant ahi, or "gorillas" as they are called in the trade. We weighed them on a dockside scale, and it was hard to ignore the open stares of other fishermen. Our most immediate concern was loading the fish into the back of a pickup truck that we had borrowed.

"Eddie" and "Freddie" weighed in at 160 and 178 lbs. respectively, and the slippery monsters initially defied every technique that we tried. After finally boarding them, to the great amusement of onlookers, we headed to the freight terminal at Hilo airport where, by pre-arrangement, DHL would fly our fish to Honolulu. We had warned our shipping agent, Sherma, to expect some trouble, but the tough little tita had a herd of brothers, the smallest of whom weighed three hundred pounds. Moreover, they were Aki's "cousins." "No worries, guys. I look aftah you fish." There was an unmistakable hint of menace in her voice, and we were happy to have her as an ally. Reassured of our cargo's safety, we had nothing to do but fly back to Honolulu and wait. The air freighter wouldn't arrive until 4:00 am.

We headed to Waikiki and strolled down Kalakaua Avenue. William eagerly pointed out some of his old haunts and the lifeguard stations where he had worked, including the infamous "Mahu Beach," frequented largely by local homosexuals. It was June, and the soft evening air was redolent with the scent of plumeria and night blooming jasmine. An orange and purple sunset, layered with streaks of turquoise and flecked with reddish gold, flared in a brilliant climax before imploding into the gathering night. Torches were lit as the first summer stars began to appear. We had dinner at a sushi joint and then caught some Hawaiian music at the Sheraton Moana. Back on the street we were propositioned by working girls, but thought the better of it. Eventually we headed to Chinatown, where evening turned to night and then the nether world of pre-dawn as we explored an endless series of sleazy bars, killing time and exhausting our meager supply of money.

By three o'clock only a handful of people were still on the streets. A few sad old men in stained white aprons emptied the restaurants of their offal while a couple of transvestite hookers continued to gamely work their corner. A sudden rain had finally stopped, and we picked our way through the neon puddles of Hotel St. as we made our way to the parking lot. Behind a dumpster some vice cops were beating up a suspect; a squad car, blue lights flashing, served as a sentinel. We hurried on.

We got to the freight terminal just in time to see DHL's ancient, sputtering DC-4 roll to a stop. Smoke poured from the inboard starboard engine; oil dripped from the cowling. This was the moment of truth. A disheveled looking pilot opened the side window of the cockpit and yelled out, "Hey, are you the guys with the damn fish? Jesus Christ." He shook his head in disgust. Eddie and Freddie had arrived.

Unfortunately, we had entirely neglected to consider a means of conveying our prize ahi. We were in a hurry since they had to be delivered under the cover of darkness. There was no choice but to wrestle them into the trunk of William's mom's Buick which we had borrowed for the evening. We secured the load with a piece of rope, but the tails stuck out a couple of feet. We were hardly discreet as we sped down Nimitz and pulled into the Suzukis' facility.

The sisters were happy to see us, as was George, offering hot coffee and malasadas, but there had been some trouble earlier that night. Someone had thrown a rock through the office window and scattered nails in the parking lot. I noticed an old .38 service revolver lying on Phyllis's desk. "We are so glad to see you boys, but we are worried about Evil Elder Brother. He is a very bad man as you can see." I was beginning to feel like we were trapped in a bad kung-fu movie.

Everyone's spirits lifted, however, with the coming dawn, and we reassured Phyllis and Gladys that we were firm in our resolve. They counted out the cash, crisp twenties, and we made plans to return to Hilo. Despite the continued threats of violence, things went pretty well for the next couple of weeks. Then one morning we found the atmosphere dramatically changed.

Both sisters were tearful, dabbing at their eyes with tissue, and yet strangely ebullient, almost giddy. Gladys spoke first. "Life is so funny. We are so confused. Mr. Mirikitani called earlier to say that Elder Brother was found floating in the harbor, dead of an apparent heart attack. He offered his condolences....we won't have to worry about the business anymore....but he was our brother....small kid days and all." She started to laugh but thought the better of it and quickly resumed her weeping. Frankly we were glad to get out of the fish business and un-conflicted about the demise of Elder Brother.

More surprising was the wedding invitation that arrived a month later. It would turn out to be a quiet, intimate affair, since Mr. Mirikitani and Gladys were far from young. George, William, and I were the only haoles invited, a distinct honor. After the ceremony and many toasts to the new couple, an invigorated Mr. M. took me aside. "You know some people think that Elder Brother's death was a little....fishy." He had consumed quite a bit of sake and laughed merrily at his own joke. "But I believe that a man embraces his own karma. Don't you agree?" I said that I certainly did and gave the old fellow a heart-felt smile and a warm handshake along with my sincere congratulations.

# CHAPTER X

THE FISH ESCAPADE HAD COME AT A FORTUNATE time. We made enough money to last until harvest, Jeb and his crew had a new business connection, and George was widely praised in the Japanese community. It was time to re-engage with the marijuana crop. In early July we returned to the woods for the first time in many weeks. Our primary mission was to "sex" the patches. That is, we had to identify and eliminate the male plants, allowing only the female plants to grow to maturation. It was critical to go to each area every seven days since plants could "declare" in that short amount of time.

After the machinations of the fish business, it was refreshing to be hiking again. We carried only day packs with food, water, clippers, a rain jacket, and extra t-shirts. Freed from the heavy weights of the spring, we fairly skipped along the trails, reveling in our freedom of motion. Entering the first patch I was pleasantly shocked. The seedlings of May were over six feet tall. William immediately began to closely examine every plant for the tell-tale beginnings of male flowers. A single male plant could easily pollinate the entire patch, and seeded pot would be practically worthless in a market that demanded sinsemilla. It was still early in the summer, so Will found only one male, although several plants looked suspicious. He said that when he first started growing pakalolo, it was hard to cut down such vibrant plants. He had to remind himself that they took up the resources (light, nutrients, water) which then became available to the females. To see all the plants we had to go twice a week, dividing our domain in half. Eventually we had to add a third day to cover "The Frontier," as we referred to our far eastern territory.

In retrospect it was the best of times. Our days were spent deep in the heart of an exotic wilderness. There was a clarity to the air, a purity to the light; colors were heightened, saturated. The air was rich with the oxygen of the breathing forest. The pluvious mornings of spring were replaced by the occasional summer shower. The once boisterous streams had quieted to cheerfully murmuring brooks. It was altogether peaceful. We never heard a helicopter, save for the occasional tourists flying high above on their way to Hana.

No jeep tracks appeared on the access roads; no gun shots signaled the presence of hunters. William counseled me to enjoy this time, since it would not last, as I well knew from the previous year. "Everyone knows when harvest approaches. Rip-offs, the Feds, Green Harvest, Makuakane and his henchmen, shopkeepers, restauranteurs, car salesmen, even schoolkids. This is it. The big casino. The only game in town unless you're a real estate developer. The money spigot is waiting to be turned on. Fortunes won and lost. Our little day hikes will become somewhat more stressful." I wondered if we would be required to defend our interests; I didn't like the idea of gun play. "Well, Sam, I would never shoot anybody if that's what you mean. On the other hand, if we had to flee, a few loud rounds might make our pursuers think twice about following us." He paused. "Then, too, you never know. Some friends had to spend the night in the woods two years ago when, coming out with a load at twilight, they saw armed brigands waiting at the top of the road. They slipped away unnoticed, but it was alarming. They waited a whole day to make sure the coast was clear— without food or shelter I might add. No, Sam, nobody is going to rob us. I feel firmly about that." There was a fierce gleam in his eye, and I didn't pursue the subject, but I wasn't entirely convinced.

My concern resurfaced, however, a couple of

days later. William received a phone call from Clayton Hong, a friend of his from Punahou days. Clayton had matriculated to Harvard and then Harvard Law. He had grown up poor in Kalihi, a depressed neighborhood in Honolulu. His parents ran a neighborhood grocery store at a time when that was still possible. Will said that he probably could have done anything in the legal profession, but he wanted to come home to Hawaii. He took the one job that was available upon his return— working for the federal prosecutor. Apparently Clayton had expressed misgivings at the time since he was a good Democrat and a champion of the underdog, but he needed a paycheck and had helped to put some really bad guys away. He was, however, very sympathetic to marijuana growers and loyal to William who, as a popular haole in high school, had befriended the slight, bespectacled Chinese boy.

His message was unsettling. A federal task force was being assembled to deal with "the marijuana problem." The Drug Enforcement Agency, Alcohol Tobacco and Firearms, and the IRS were all a part of the team. They planned to concentrate on Maui and the Big Island. Clayton was cryptic but promised to call again when he knew more.

William's response was surprisingly measured, which I knew concealed a deep concern. "This isn't good at all. The local cops know the game.

They try to rip us off, but they aren't about to kill the goose that lays the golden egg, as it were. The Feds, though, might be interested in prosecution. I wonder if Nancy Reagan is behind this." To be a pot grower was one thing, but to be a convicted felon was quite another. As I had in the past, I once again expressed my consternation to W. "Don't worry, Sam. You can literally run out the back door if anything comes down. You don't own property, you don't have a family, you don't even have a Hawaii driver's license. As far as anyone could tell, you're just a visitor from Connecticut."

As I had hoped, my performance at the poetry reading greatly enhanced my standing with Maile. I upbraided myself for not coming clean about the circumstances surrounding that evening, but then, I rationalized, maybe her adulation was not undeserved. With my fish money I was able to squire her with a certain amount of style. I think that I had obviously developed a self-inflated view of myself. She turned heads at any restaurant or event, yet there was an absence of pretense in her demeanor. She had a natural grace, refined, perhaps, by years of hula training. I had managed a prolonged kiss, but received none of the customary signals that would have encouraged me to go further. When I apprised William of the situation, he cautioned me that she was probably a relative innocent. "No doubt she had a few lovers in college, but she is an ambitious young woman who was certainly fully engaged in athletics and her studies. It's not like it was in our day, Sam. I mean people our age are still promiscuous, given the proper circumstances of course, but the young people coming out of college are much more serious—and cautious. This AIDS business is disturbing. It even gives me pause, although sometimes I wonder if it isn't just a Republican conspiracy to scare people away from sex. Maybe you need to find someone less.... insular, less provincial. You know this windsurfing thing is really changing the female landscape."

The next day we went on an exploratory mission to Kanaha beach, the epicenter of the new sport. The parking lot was filled with "Maui cruisers," beat up old cars that were festooned with equipment loaded on top, masts sticking out like so many proboscises. It was apparent that that the value of the gear far exceeded that of the vehicles. It was early afternoon and the grassy area adjacent to the beach was littered with brightly colored sails and boards. The amiable chatter was entirely confined to a discussion of wind conditions, expected wind conditions, appropriate sail size, who was going out, who was just coming in.

There was a bustle, a firmness of intent, as men and women busily rigged up. There was a noticeable lack of conversation about anything other than the task at hand. We positioned ourselves on the beach and watched the happy flock take flight, one after another, while William rolled a joint. A few beginners were struggling to learn to "beach start," a maneuver that entailed holding the boom correctly and letting the sail fill while jumping on the moving board. The more accomplished windsurfers sped toward the shore, jibed quickly, and accelerated away on the opposite tack.

Will was delivering a lazy running commentary on the various women coming and going, when he suddenly sat up straight and nudged me with an elbow. "Samuel, pay attention, you must witness this, the emergence of Aphrodite, 'out of the sea green foam,' a phrase from Blake I believe." Before us, coming in to perch at water's edge and make a minor adjustment to her sail, was an impossibly beautiful woman. I asked Will if he knew her. "No, Sam, I don't know her, but we've met. She is the Australian champion, or something like that. Hangs out at Hoʻokipa sometimes." He blew a lung full of smoke skyward, as if in offering, and appeared thoughtful. I felt that he was about to deliver a disquisition, and I was not disappointed. "You see, Sam, she is an archetype, which is the most necessary quality of a goddess. That is to say, her physical proportions conform to a universal, almost mathematical ideal. Her proportions are perfect. Her legs are long and long all the way through her buttocks. Some women have legs that are long alright, but the ankles can be somewhat truncated. Not so with Aphrodite. That exquisite extension goes right through to her big toe. More amazing is her perfect ass. Two high, tight globes perfectly rounded. Her trunk is muscular, hinting at considerable abdominal strength, but without the blatant ostentation of the gym enthusiast. Her arms and shoulders are well defined, suggesting an integrated musculature. Her blonde hair, naturally highlighted by the sun, is authentic. I know because I once noted the color of her pubic patch, that golden flocculus of fleece, as it broached the narrow confines of her bikini. In conversation one is arrested by her unblinking, luminescent blue eyes. They sparkle with humor one moment, but can harden to an adamantine glint. One feels like he is being appraised as a jungle cat would size up potential prey or perhaps a future mate. An aquiline nose and intelligent forehead complete the portrait."

"Does she have a boyfriend?" I asked the obvious question.

"I have often seen her at the beach but never in the company of a man. This separateness is perhaps what makes her a goddess more than anything. She is un-compromised, insouciant. Each of us is allowed to liberally indulge in his own fantasy. To be with a man would make her commonplace, and yet we all, her admirers, want to be that man. She is a vessel for our hopes, and our inspiration."

"You have obviously given this a great deal of thought," I said, accepting the joint in turn.

"Certainly. What's the point of being educated otherwise? We both took Segal's course in college. In classical mythology the gods and goddesses lived among us, interacting with humans, but without the moral constraints, the mores, that mortals were subject to. They were powerful, they were capricious. What seemed like cruelty was really only indifference."

"So Aphrodite here has descended from the celestial firmament? Alighting at Kanaha on the gossamer wings of a nylon sail?"

"Oh Sam, don't be a kill joy. If I am to resume my writing I need a Muse. Don't we all? I believe you've found yours in Maile. It is easy to satisfy ourselves but necessarily harder to please a Muse. Beauty is requisite, of course, but that is her least interesting attribute. Without the faculty of critical intelligence her judgement is empty. We strive to please her and sublimate our desire to perfect our art. Her beauty is only symbolic, a reminder of our insufficiencies. She is enigmatic, a hierophant. She is the original audience, and we must believe that she has a soft spot in her heart, a quality of empathy. Without that her ridicule would be crushing."

"I grant you that gods and goddesses are, indeed, human-like but with a different attitude. So, what is her....attitude?"

"Well, I've gotten some good vibrations."

"Ok. I can see where this is going. It's one thing to have piece of strange in New York, but quite another on a very small island. You married a goddess!"

"Wives can't be goddesses. Their concerns are mundane, quotidian—diapers, bills, in-laws, play groups, yoga class. The Muse only requires a commitment to Art."

"William, your dissimulation is so transparent."

"Really?" He actually seemed surprised, maybe because he was stoned.

"Yes, really. You put me in the position of playing the prig when I only have your best interests at heart. Your concupiscence is a danger. Is Aphrodite to be your hetaera? Laura is a goddess, one with uxorial concerns admittedly, but a goddess nonetheless—a goddess of the hearth, of fertility, of regeneration." There was a silence as Will digested my outburst. Then he smiled a goofy grin.

"Sam, you are my brother, and I have always valued your insight, ever since college. That's one reason I wanted you to come out here. But you have to admit Aphrodite is a piece of work."

I conceded the point and admitted that he had always had great taste in women. "So let's go see what the in-house goddess is cooking for dinner." As we stood up to go, Aphrodite glanced back at us to make sure we were looking, acknowledged us with a secret smile, jumped on her board and quickly disappeared, racing toward the surf line.

# CHAPTER XI

WE RETURNED HOME TO A BEE HIVE OF activity. Several moms had gathered with their progeny to get ready for the rodeo parade the next morning. July Fourth fell in the middle of the week that year, so the festivities were moved to the following weekend. William seemed grumpy at the prospect but felt that it was important for me to witness a quintessentially local event. As we sat down at the kitchen table with our bottles of beer, a horse's head appeared, inserting itself through the open window. An explanation quickly followed as an excited Laurie haltered the animal and began to lead him away. "Isn't this great!" she cried out. "Can you believe it? Old Man Perreira was going to sell him to the Tongans for their luau! I found out from his son and said that I would pay the hundred bucks. The kids love him. He is so gentle." Laurie in her enthusiasm reminded me of a great sunflower. She had an open, round face that dimpled when she smiled and merry eyes that sparkled above a freckled nose. William's coy windsurfing avatar did not, to my mind, compare favorably. In the small pasture behind the house, the neighborhood children clambered over the patient creature while Laura stroked his nose. Stryder ran around in circles yelling "Horsey! Horsey!"

There were plenty of "horseys" in evidence the next day in Makawao. Laurie insisted that we get to town early in order to secure a good viewing spot. An early cloud cover dissipated and gave way to brilliant sunshine. A happy crowd of spectators lined Baldwin Ave., engaged in animated conversation, decked out in their best western wear. Even Will had succumbed and donned his best alligator skin boots and his most soiled cowboy hat. He hoisted Stryder up on his shoulders as the distant sound of brass instruments signaled the beginning of the review.

The parade was a chance for Maui's equine enthusiasts to display themselves and their mounts before an adoring home town crowd. There were, in addition, numerous floats, decorated pickup trucks, high school marching bands, politicians with fixed, false smiles waving from rented convertibles, a samba troupe, the young rodeo queen and her court, veterans in full uniform, and a phalanx of hot rods, the pride of the old timers who drove them. I knew that Maile was planning to ride in the parade, and when she appeared she drew the focus of the crowd, a regal figure seated atop a beautiful paint. She and her horse were both draped with flower lei and were followed by three other local girls on gleaming steeds, tail and manes combed out, their tack oiled and polished. Each rider gave queenly, compact waves to the crowd as their horses instinctively wove from one side of the street to the other, heads held high. The horses enjoyed the adoration as much as their owners and seemed to understand the role they played in the pageant. As I looked down Baldwin Avenue at the ramshackle buildings with their old west style false fronts, draped in corny patriotic bunting and American flags, and the excited throngs in their rodeo attire, I felt that I was viewing a scene from a different epoch. Save for a few modern cars, it could have been the 1950s or the 1930s, or even earlier. At that moment Makawao seemed hopelessly charming and precious. Unfortunately William didn't share my enthusiasm. He was still a little peevish and dismissed the proceedings out of hand, a curmudgeon in his thirties. "Things were different when I moved here in the 70s, Sam. Everybody knew each other; there was a sense of community. We've been invaded by rich people who have little empathy for, or understanding of, local paniolo culture. They might don the proper outfits, put on their fancy boots, but they don't know how to ride or rope. The only thing they can saddle is the front seat of a BMW." I demurred. It seemed like a wonderfully authentic event, with representatives from every race and sub-culture. As I spoke the hippy samba band came into view and filled the air with the sound of steel drums. Scantily clad women strutted and gyrated in the July heat. Next came the middle school ukulele club, clad in identical aloha wear, strumming in perfect unison, their voices lifting in pubescent tenor. Miss Maui followed on a float, crowned with a tiara of sparkling costume jewelry. Then more horses, seemingly unaffiliated, loosely grouped, Next, a Hawaiian group, the something or rather ali'i, bare chested, wearing stern, martial expressions and helmets of feathers. A county councilman waving from the back of a pickup truck drew good natured jeers. A herd of freakishly small miniature ponies followed, driven like sheep by a fat lady. The Kaupakalua roping club passed, well mounted, with, what else, ropes hanging from their pommels. A '53 Willys hot rod had expired and was being pushed by willing bystanders. Another politician, an avowed environmentalist and popular favorite, was cheered enthusiastically. More horses, one of which was prancing nervously and rearing under the unsteady hand of its rider. A mule drawn wagon, filled with special needs kids, advanced slowly. The kids responded to the affectionate roar of the crowd by wildly waving their hats, grinning like jack o'lanterns. Now a reggae band on the back of a flat bed, powered up by a noisy generator. In its wake, children from the Hongwanji pre-school "riding" broomstick horses. And finally the shit brigade, in clown costumes, sweeping up horse manure. "No, Sam, you're right," admitted William, smiling at the spectacle before him. "This is still an honest, wonderful expression of our community. I just feel that now, in the 1980s, we are at a tipping point, and I worry that our beloved institutions will be subverted, swept away, by a tsunami of mainlanders. I'm glad you're here now. We might be at the beginning of the end of an era." I remarked that the rusticity of Makawao certainly seemed to be intact. "Sam, look over at the General Store where all the tourists are. When I worked for the Park Service, our crew would come back from a ten day work trip in the Haleakala National Park—unwashed, unshaven, our jeans stiff with dirt—throw our saddles in a heap, stack our rifles, order a case of beer, and hold court, catching up with friends and neighbors. What would happen now? You would probably be arrested. That's what I mean. Subtle changes can be profound. Back then everybody knew who we were." I slyly suggested that windsurfing seemed to have given a bit of a lift to the North Shore, energetically anyway. "True enough. We've become a bit more cosmopolitan, and I applaud that. An invigorating dose of hipness is a good thing. I just worry about the slow, glacial, ineluctable momentum that will overwhelm our little island. What will this place be like in twenty years, thirty? The mess that is Oahu should serve as a cautionary tale."

The actual rodeo began in the early afternoon at the Oskie Rice Arena, a mile or so below William's property. The large pasture next to the arena was covered with hundreds of vehicles, including many large trucks pulling horse trailers. Will told me that although this was very much a local event, cowboys from around the state were increasingly attracted to what was becoming Hawaii's premier rodeo. Laurie had saved us a place in the bleachers, having arrived much earlier. She was surrounded by her friends and all their children who were busy slurping their shave ice. She looked radiant and completely at home in tight jeans, red boots, and a slightly unbuttoned western shirt with pearl fastenings. Her thick blonde hair was neatly plaited and hung in a long pigtail beneath her straw hat.

She had grown up on a small ranch east of Santa Barbara, and to her the smell of "horse manure and cow shit was an elixir."

Uncle Dave was there giving the little boys a simulated bull ride on his knee, mimicking the histrionic announcer in the booth. Jonas wouldn't be coming, we learned, because he thought the whole "circus" ridiculous and merely celebrated cruelty to animals. William chose to cast a critical eye on the contestants, only once allowing that a team of calf ropers was "pretty good." He thought that the horses were better athletes than their riders. I told him that he was, again, being peevish. To me the cowboys performed amazing feats with consummate skill. "Sam, I've alluded to my childhood, but I will remind you that I spent a lot of time in Oklahoma where my mom is from. I used to hate being taken away from the beach in June, when all my friends were surfing Waikiki. It was only for a month or so, which seems like a long time when you're a kid, but I came to appreciate my time there. My aunt was very laissez-faire when it came to child management. She had a big ranch, still does, and my cousins and I would often spend an entire day riding our horses through the countryside. All the neighbors knew us, and we let ourselves through their pastures. We'd fish in creek bottoms, go skinny dipping, shoot rattlesnakes with our .22s, chase cattle, and gallop our horses 'til they foamed with lather. There was a little crossroads country store that kept Dr. Peppers on ice, which we could put on account. In the evening the adults would gather on the screened in porch with their cocktails and watch the heat lightning flicker against distant thunderheads, never even bothering to ask us about our day."

"Well that sounds wonderfully idyllic, but what's the point?"

"The point, Sam, is that Oklahoma is to rodeo as Hawaii is to surfing. People there live it every day on their ranches. Ok, maybe I've been too harsh in my criticism, but that's part of the fun. Some of the guys are quite talented; I just see details that you don't. I will say that the horses are getting better every year. A lot of them are brought in from the mainland now."

Looking over at Will in profile with his dark good looks and high cheek bones, I was able to easily detect the Native American contribution to his gene pool. "So, did your dad ever go with you?"

"On a rare occasion, but I'm sure that he enjoyed time off from my sisters and me. He and his buddies could surf and carouse without the constraints of domesticity. And of course he had a large, prominent company to run with many employees and attendant responsibilities. His family came to Hawaii in the 1880s, so he's into being kama'aina in a way that seems a little ridiculous to mom. He calls her the Comanche Princess, and she calls him Jungle James. They do seem to love each other, but everybody needs a break."

"When was the last time you were there?"

"Oh, it's been many years, but I understand cousin Alice is engaged, and I will attend her wedding, whenever that might be. Shoot, Sam, maybe I can wangle you an invite. Come see the real America. Get some ribs at Bob's Barbeque, go drinkin' at the Tattle Tail, put some Merle Haggard on the juke box, drag Main on a Saturday night. And those country girls are hot; they grew up with breeding, they know when a mare's in heat. Here's an expression for you—a stallion 'covers' a mare. Ain't that quaint?"

At this point there was a hiatus in the proceedings as the coliseum (as I had come to think of it) was being prepared for the bull riding. I caught a glimpse of Maile and a couple of her friends who were leaning on the rail about thirty yards away. I was about to make my way down when I saw that the attention of the young women was being diverted by a handsome Portuguese-Hawaiian cowboy with a number on his back—presumably a contestant in the featured event. I experienced a pang of jealousy which surprised me. After all I had exercised the predilection of horny youth and had some success in Lahaina with a couple of tourist girls. The encounters were not all that memorable save for one great line from a buxom Canadian gal who, while on top, said, "You can milk my titties by sucking on them," before grabbing a pendulous breast and thrusting it into my mouth. Affecting a casual tone I nudged Will and asked who the fellow was.

"Oh, that's Cody 'Bully' De Rego, our star bull rider. He actually put in some time on the mainland, Wyoming I think. A good guy and quite the ladies' man as you can see." I did see and asked Will if he knew him. "We're casual friends. Years ago I couldn't find my gloves right before I was called, and he loaned me his. He was just a teenager then."

"You rode bulls?" I was astonished. That seemed like complete madness.

"Well, yes, I was young, in my twenties. It was before the pot thing had taken off. Hey, I once won a buckle and a thousand dollars. Big money back then." He laughed.

"At least you were wise enough to quit."

"Wise? I don't know about that. I got badly hurt. It took years to truly recover, and you've probably noticed that I'm still a little gimpy at the end of the day. But it could have been worse, I got stomped pretty good."

My gaze wandered back to Maile, and I consoled myself that she was only one of several women being charmed by "Bully." William read my thoughts which were obvious from my countenance.

He seemed to take inordinate pleasure from my discomfort. "Ah, my poor Lotherio. The great philanderer, the Casanova of Lahaina, is jealous. Now who's the rake? Come on, Samuel, you told me all about the Bavarian milk maid."

"She was Canadian."

"Whatever. Listen, he's not her type. He's country, and she's a sophisticate. They probably went to elementary school together."

"You were the one in college who always lectured me about the animal impulses of women, claiming that there was an anthropological bias toward the rugged male, the hunter, the killer. You cited a study of paleo-Native American skulls that revealed that forty percent died of wounds to the skull, the hypothesis being that they fought over females."

"Wow, Sam. Really? Well, it's true that we haven't evolved all that much, but still I think that there has to be an intellectual component. After all, smart cave men could always outwit the dullards."

Our conversation was interrupted by the impresario on the overly loud p.a. system who was pleased to recognize one of this year's rodeo sponsors. "Ladies and gentlemen let's give a big Makawao welcome to Big Island rancher Lincoln Makuakane." The inevitable convertible emerged from behind a gate. Perched above the back seat was a large Hawaiian man dressed in a long sleeved aloha shirt and black cowboy hat. He was built like a lineman, with a hard, prosperous gut hanging over his belt. His smile, even at a distance, seemed strangely malevolent. His driver, another big man with wrap around sunglasses, remained sullen. As he made his way around the perimeter, there was a very faint ripple of applause. I recognized the name and then remembered what Will had told me about him.

"Very good, Sam. Yes, that's the Big Island Rancher alright, head of a far reaching criminal syndicate and perhaps the most powerful man in the state. Gambling, prostitution, extortion, labor racketeering, you name it, he's got a hand in it. And lately, of course, his attention has turned to the pakalolo industry. Every politician pays him tribute, the Democrats anyway. The few Republicans are irrelevant old stuffed shirt haoles that nobody pays any attention to. I do have to wonder why he's here. He usually doesn't expose himself; he has plenty of minions that represent him in his affairs. Maybe he just wants to be the Big Man of the moment, simple narcissism. Or maybe he's trying to remind someone of his influence. There are plenty of politicos here."

"So is he the enemy?"

"Well, he's one of them. As I told you, he directs the local cops during Green Harvest. Everything they rip off is processed at his ranch on the Big Island. I think I'll call Clayton and find out what he knows."

I eventually made my way to Maile's side, and she greeted me with a kiss to the cheek before returning her attention to the arena. "We're waiting to see Bully. He's next up out of chute number three. Oh, these are my friends Gloria and Iwi." The gate swung open as promised, and Bully artfully rode the twisting, turning beast, successfully beating the eight second buzzer. He dismounted with a deft, athletic flourish that had the girls cheering. "Wasn't that great Sam!" I had to admit that it was an impressive display, but quickly changed the subject to Maile's novel. We made a date to look over the latest chapter.

# CHAPTER XII

IT WAS BACK TO BUSINESS AFTER THE RODEO
weekend. William had devised a novel way
of accessing the woods. We would ride up on
mountain bikes, posing as sportsmen, wearing
bike shorts and helmets and vested with assorted
accoutrement. Once there we could hide our bikes,
change into work clothes, and go about our business, reversing the process in the evening. This
afforded us a convenient cover and eliminated the
necessity of the pre-dawn drop off. As a plus it
gave us the opportunity to pursue a long forgotten
boyish pleasure. I thought we looked suspicious;
Dave thought we looked "gay" in our spandex
shorts. Fortunately we were unmolested, encoun-
tering only a couple of biologists from the UH
who were conducting a study of native birds. We
stopped and conversed at length with them before

continuing on our jaunt. Our disguise seemed to be effective.

We paused at the edge of the forest to look for "magic" mushrooms in the Haleakala Ranch pasture. They often emerged from cow shit after a rain and contained psilocybin, a psychedelic ingredient. I had never tried one, but the guys assured me that it was a "good trip," not as heavy as LSD. We found quite a few, including the prized bullet shaped variety. My partners didn't hesitate to eat them, but I found the taste repellant and had to choke down a couple with a water chaser.

Sure enough, about forty-five minutes later I began to feel the effects. I fought an initial wave of nausea but then felt wonderfully light on my feet. I had to suppress an impulse to simply run down the mountain. The morning sun flickered through dew-heavy trees that sparkled with refracted light. I became intensely aware of the oxygen flooding my system and marveled at the steady pulse of a muscular heart. I weighed the contradictory feelings of being at once ephemeral and at the same time indestructible and powerful. I wished for wings, for I was flying.

Skipping down the jeep trail, I tripped over a tree root and did a full forward roll. Sitting up I examined myself and started to laugh. Will, who was behind me, couldn't contain himself and laughed until tears rolled down his face. Dave and

Jonas were like-wise afflicted. When we recovered we decided to treat ourselves to a swim in a large pool that was at the base of a waterfall about a quarter mile up a narrow valley. Even though it was summer, there was still a good volume of running water. We let the water pound our backs, an excellent massage, and then cavorted in the swimming hole before lying on the hot, sun heated rocks surrounding it. Eventually we reluctantly got dressed and addressed ourselves to the mission. "Quite the summer camp!" quipped Will. "People would pay top dollar just to hang out with us."

Late that afternoon we hiked back up the mountain so that we could recover our bikes and then ride down to Olinda Road and so on to home. Laurie had prepared a big meal, cheerfully called us reprobates, and set out dinner on the deck. We were still in the delightful stage of a trip that we called "afterglow." After yet another cold beer, we smoked a post-prandial cheroot and revisited my hilarious prat fall, evoking laughter once again. Writing in my diary that night, I attempted to recall the day and kept using a word that I try to avoid—"magical."

An hour or so after bedtime, a ringing phone disturbed the night's peace. Laurie's friend Rebecca called to say that her husband Tom, a fellow pot grower, had not returned home. She was worried. Did we know anything? William counseled her that he was probably ok, but to call back in the early morning. It is hard to imagine now, but this was in an era before cell phones were ubiquitous or even invented. If an accident were to befall someone in the woods, there would be no way for him to communicate his predicament.

At dawn a distraught Becca reported that Tom had still not returned. Laurie implored William to do something. Although we were utterly exhausted from the previous day's exertions, our duty was clear—Will would organize a search party. He knew roughly the area in which Tom and his partner worked. Tom had gone on a solo hike while Jim was off-island, so there was no one on hand to give specific guidance. Their patches were in the lowlands, and Will knew from a previous discussion the approximate dimensions of their territory. David and Jonas were recruited along with Aki and his cousin Koa. Each team of two was assigned a valley and would begin upslope and follow the stream down the mountain. A gunshot would signal that Tom had been found.

After the cool upcountry air, the lowlands seemed unbearably hot and humid. By noon we were utterly depleted by the rough terrain. William pulled out a ration of cocaine which he claimed that he had hidden away for just such an emergency. Thus fortified we plunged on, hoping for a signal from one of the others, but by late

afternoon we had heard nothing. At the rendezvous point the mood was grim. It was obvious
to all of us that something dire had happened to
Tom. There was nothing to do but rest and recon-
vene in the morning. Back home we discovered a
note from Laurie saying that she and Stryder were
at Rebecca's, offering what comfort she could.
Becca and Tom had a little baby girl, Gwendolyn.

The next day we were up again at dawn. William decided to bring Harry, the intuitive pitbull,
along with us. That dog always seemed to know
what was required of him, and as we reconnoi-
tered the valley once again, he kept his nose to the
ground, occasionally bounding off to check out a
new lead. Will had let him smell an old shirt of
Tom's, and we occasionally refreshed his memory.

By mid-morning Search and Rescue had been
alerted, and their little yellow helicopter flitted
about, sometimes disappearing behind a ridge and
then reappearing down by the coast, or climbing
high to get an overview. Of course it was a little
unnerving to be under the scrutiny of a chopper,
and they undoubtedly discovered many of Tom
and Jim's patches. We pressed on into the late
afternoon. If Tom was badly injured or unconscious, his chances of survival would diminish
with every passing hour. Halting at the top of a
precipitous waterfall, we peered over the edge and

saw him, face down, in a pool of water eighty feet below. His pack was still on his back.

While Will made his way down to the body, I scrambled up the steep valley wall and found a flat bit of pasture, waving a white t-shirt to attract the attention of Search and Rescue. By the time they spotted me, it was dusk. I pointed them in the general direction and yelled for William who responded with a gun shot. I found out later that the S and R crew had told Will that they couldn't accommodate him and me in the helicopter—it would be over gross weight. Will replied that in that case they could find their own way out of the valley without his guidance. It was dark and they relented. The next day a coroner determined that Tom had not died from the fall itself, but had drowned in the pool.

The service for Tom was a community event. Most of the attendees and their families were pakalolo farmers. There were a few that even William didn't know. Tibetan prayer flags fluttered in the afternoon breeze as a Hawaiian priest intoned a mournful chant. People took turns addressing the small crowd, remembering Tom and offering their own prayers. Two young women with guitars sang beautifully and finished a musical tribute by leading us all in singing "Nearer My God to Thee." As we finished the last chorus, a summer rain shower higher up the mountain produced a brilliant rainbow of unusual intensity that quickly faded before vanishing, as fleeting as life itself. No one spoke for several minutes. The only sound was muted crying and the rustle of wind in the trees. I looked at Will and was surprised to see tears silently rolling down his cheeks. Rebecca took the urn containing Tom's ashes and tossed them in the air. A sudden gust bore them up and away in a small vortex. Tom was gone.

A wake followed in the proper Irish tradition. Tom's parents and siblings had flown in for the service, and they were profoundly touched by the outpouring of affection for their son and brother. Alcohol stimulated the sentimentality of the occasion, and there was frequent loud laughter which would have been unseemly just two hours before. Everybody had a Tom story to tell, and his relatives hung on every word, interjecting well received anecdotes about his early childhood misadventures. Later I saw Will and Dad, each with an arm around the other's shoulder, quietly talking apart from the crowd. Will organized all the growers and easily extracted from each a promise to contribute a small percentage of his harvest to a fund for Rebecca and little Gwendolyn. It was all we could do. I saw then the profound power of community and realized how much we harried urbanites had lost. Here was a tribe, an extended family, coming together in a rite as old as humankind to support each other and mourn a lost member. At that moment I knew that I, too, belonged, and that I had found something I hadn't even realized was missing.

# CHAPTER XIII

IN OUR PATCHES WE FOUND AND ELIMINATED increasing numbers of male plants. I was carefully instructed on how to identify an early male, and my patient tutors would sometimes allow me to "sex" a patch and then review my work. One day I saw my first silver hair on a seven foot beauty—an early female, a harbinger. Inexorably we moved closer to harvest.

That same week Will's friend Clayton called to say that he was coming to Maui with his girlfriend for a golfing vacation. Would we like to meet them in Ka'anapali? Naturally, Will was eager to hear Clay's report on the Federal Task Force. The conference took place at an outdoor bar under the shade of a beach umbrella. Clayton was not as I had pictured him. I think frankly that I expected a caricature of a Chinese man. Instead he was trim and fit, well turned out in expensive slacks and a

Brooks Brothers polo shirt. Tasseled loafers and horned rim glasses complemented his look. Mimi, his Asian fiance, was not a local girl but a Radcliffe graduate from Boston. We ordered margaritas all around and spent a good twenty minutes in random conversation before Clayton brought the meeting to order. "Will, I don't need to emphasize that all this is strictly confidential."

"Ok, Clayton, I'll take notes on this napkin and then eat it."

"I'm serious. They'd have my ass if anyone found out I was aiding and abetting a suspect, a possible perp."

"Sorry, Clay....suspect?"

"In brief, the task force has compiled a dossier of all known or alleged pot growers. Your name is included. They know that in order to prosecute they are going to have to place you in the same domicile as the contraband. Going after people in the woods won't work. There is no law against hiking." He paused and signaled the waitress for another round. "So, above all, you don't want to process or store anything at all in your house. Make sure it's as clean as a whistle. Don't even leave a roach in the ashtray. And, if you have any unregistered firearms, bury them." Clayton's stark warnings temporarily interjected a note of solemnity into our little get together.

"Well, I guess we'll have to rent a drying house."

"Be discrete about it. Some DEA types are already on Maui, attempting to integrate themselves into the community." Clayton chuckled. "But they are so obviously narcs! The woman dresses up like a 60s hippy, and the man wears starched aloha shirts—tucked in!—and has affected a sparse mustache. Quite risible, actually. Now here's the interesting thing. They, the Feds, are at odds with local law enforcement. Maui and Big Island cops are only giving nominal support to to the project because, as you know, they want to rip off the pot in the woods. It is unlikely that all the agencies will act in concert. Of course Makuakane is the great Oz, carefully orchestrating things from behind his curtain. The police chief on Maui looks the other way, for a cut I'm sure, while the head of Vice, Randall Toguchi, an acne scarred, whiskey besotted creep, actually heads things up on the ground for Makuakane. The good news is they don't give a shit about arresting you."

"But the Feds do?"

"Certainly. There is some real money behind this effort, and they need to show some results."

"So, whom are they going to go after first?"

"I guess that depends on what intelligence they can gather."

The sun was just above the horizon and cast a blinding light that shimmered on the ocean's surface. The balmy air was occasionally stirred by a zephyr from the dying trade winds, while out on the golden sands honeymooning couples stood holding hands, waiting to see our familiar burning star sink behind the edge of the earth. The margaritas were potent, the summer evening heaven sent, and yet we were discussing a matter of serious import with its ramifications of potential disaster. In retrospect I should have been more worried than I was, but the tequila numbed my concerns, and I concentrated on feeling the pleasurable warmth from the last rays of the sun. It occurred to me then that that it would be perfect time to bail out of the pot growing enterprise. I had been a big help to Will, I had experienced Maui, school would resume in September, and, above all, I wouldn't have to face a federal felony charge, a sure detriment to my law career. Why I chose to remain was easy enough to explain at the time. There was the money, of course, but that was abstract, a mere promise, a tantalizing chimera. More compelling was my loyalty to William and his disappointment in me if I should quit. Then there was Maile. I couldn't imagine how that would turn out, but I knew that it was unlikely that I would ever again enjoy the company of such a beautiful woman. The island itself had started to exert a powerful hold on me. I was another bewitched sailor, jumping ship to escape the frigid northern winters. Yes, I would stay, but a prescient sense of impending trouble would prove to be unfortunately accurate. Later I would view the experience as part of the myth that I would create for myself, a manly rite of passage, a chance to bond with fellow hunters as we sharpened our spear points around a roaring fire, tearing off chunks of roasting mastodon while recalling tales of the hunt with loud exclamations, furious hand gestures, and happy grunts of approval. The women hang back at the edges, their eyes sparkling with amazement at the stories, feeling the pulse of lust in their loins as they imagine being impaled by their muscular troglodytes. A nest of furs and a willing female await the successful provider. Thus it has always been. But the stories must first be ritually repeated, each re-telling adding color and detail. Finally, as the coals dim, couples retire into the darkness, there to rut like the primitives they are.

A loud voice snapped me awake. "Hey, Sam, you're drifting off." It was William tapping me on the shoulder. "Pay attention, Sam. After all you are my de facto attorney."

Clayton continued. "You told me that you saw Makuakane at the rodeo. He probably came over to make sure the county government doesn't interfere with his plans, or to offer any more than minimal co-operation with the Feds."

"When can we expect this all to happen?"

"You know better than I. The cops will hit

the crop when it's largely ready. Isn't that usually in mid-September? The Feds will try to monitor them, so I suspect Makuakane's guys will throw the DEA a bone to lead them off the scent. Of course if the U.S. Government was serious about prosecution, they would go after Makuakane, but we all know that's not politically feasible. Did you happen to notice another big man with the Big Island Rancher? His 'driver' perhaps?"

"Was he Chinese-Hawaiian? A quintessential thug?"

"That's Biggy Chun, his top lieutenant. We think Biggy committed at least three murders, but in the end we had to settle for a racketeering charge. He did five years in Halawa Prison and just got out. I put him away myself." Will's face revealed his consternation.

"He would not be a good enemy to have."

"Most definitely. But in a sense I did him a favor by agreeing to a plea deal. I know it cost the Syndicate a fortune in legal fees. He was represented by an old kama'aina white shoe law firm whose partners are chummy with the judicial branch."

I excused myself, not feeling at all well. I lay down in the still warm sand. I few minutes later Will sat down beside me. "Are you ok, Samuel? We have dinner reservations at Longhi's."

"Murder?"

"Sam, nobody's going to murder us."

"Anybody capable of murder wouldn't think twice about employing some strong arm tactics."

"I grant the point, but as I have told you, Makuakane and his henchmen have a vested interest in maintaining the status quo. They don't want any publicity; they don't want to roil the waters. They don't want to inflict violence on anyone. They just want to steal our pot."

"You don't think that they would be capable of kicking down the door of a drying house?"

"Capable, sure. But by then they'll be drying all the pot they can handle on the Big Island. Hopefully it won't be ours. I'm more worried about the jacked up, buzz cut, flak jacket wearing, ex-military agents of the Federal government."

"I'm greatly relieved," I replied facetiously.

"Good. In that case let's go join Clay and Mimi for dinner."

# CHAPTER XIV

JULY ALSO MARKED THE RE-CHRISTENING OF THE Double Barrel, the guys' 32 foot catamaran. It had been in dry dock for months, waiting for a re-fit that William was at last able to afford with some of his fish money. With fresh paint on top and below and new rigging, she danced like a thoroughbred on her mooring, twitching with every slight change in the wind. Will was anxious to try a new mainsail that he had commissioned, and we awaited its completion at the sail loft before beginning what he referred to as "sea trials."

I was excited at the prospect of sailing in Hawaii. I had often crewed on my Uncle Charlie's racing sloop which he kept in Mystic, Connecticut. We sailed primarily in Long Island Sound, but frequently visited Nantucket and once went as far as Nova Scotia. Warm water sailing was something I had always dreamed of.

When the new sail was finished, we were all eager to see how well Double Barrel would perform. We agreed to meet David and Jonas at the beach with the dinghy, and predictably everyone ran a little late. Beer was mandatory, as well as ice and food. We made another stop for gasoline and then dropped by the marine supply store for spare shackles and assorted extra parts. By the time we got everything loaded into the zodiak, it was already mid-morning, and the trade winds had begun to pick up.

The mooring was close to shore where the wind was no more than a faint breeze. Miles away, in the Pailolo Channel between Maui and Moloka'i, white caps were clearly visible. Dave remarked that it appeared to be "blowing pretty good," and shot a questioning glance at Will who was busy hanking on the jib. He looked up and stared at the distant wind line. "Yeah, the marine forecast is calling for winds of 25 to 30 knots in the channels, and they've issued a small craft warning. I don't know....well, we're here. We can reef the main and poke our nose into the channel and beat a retreat if it's too much."

"Sounds like a plan, Captain." Dave snapped a mock salute. Jonas was oblivious to the conversation. He was already stretched out on the trampoline between the hulls, basking in the sun. I was paying attention, however. Back east, vigorous white caps were a signal to head for the nearest harbor. I expressed my concern to the crew. Will acknowledged my point of view. "The thing is, Sam, at this time of year it's always windy, hence the windsurfing craze, but we are used to these conditions and have spent years sailing in these waters." I pretended to be placated but still felt a little trepidatious. When we at last came off the mooring, the wind line had shifted noticeably closer.

Initially a very light convective wind blew aft from Lahaina, and we approached the channel wing and wing, tracing only a slight wake. The shear line was soon only a few hundred yards away, a clearly visible delineation. We entered a transitional zone at its edge where the wind swirled about in random gusts. With a hundred yards to go, Will shouted out "Get ready!" sheeted in the main and cleated the traveler. Dave manned the jib. A minute passed and then the wind hit with full force, The sails snapped, we heeled over, and the Double Barrel shot forward. William was at the tiller, a wild, happy gleam in his eyes. Jonas was startled into wakefulness as water poured over the tramp. Will explained our strategy. We would sail as close to the wind as possible for some time before tacking and heading back on a broad reach. "Then, Sam, you will see what she can really do!"

It was a wet ride heading into the swells. William would fall off ever so slightly when we encountered one, easing Double Barrel over rather than attacking head on. Still, the drop on the backside was often considerable. I had to admire the design of the boat; its big flared bows were made for Hawaiian waters. I began to relax as my confidence in the boat grew. The four of us assembled behind the windscreen and popped open some beers. Jonas successfully sparked a joint. We settled into an easy rhythm, interrupted by the occasional extra heavy plunge which covered us with salt spray and caused Double Barrel to shudder. The wind shrieked in the rigging.

In mid-channel it was time to come about. William explained that cats were harder to tack than monohulls, so often they had to back the jib in order to push the bows across the wind. He ruled out a jibe as too dangerous for the conditions. When all of us were poised for the maneuver, Will called out "Ready about. Helms-a-lee!" Dave and I held out the jib; Double Barrel wavered and then slowly came around to the opposite tack. We released the sail which popped and filled. Will let out the traveler and sheeted in the main. I had been impressed by the speed of the boat close-hauled, but this was altogether different. Double Barrel quivered and hummed with the rising pitch of a banshee. The Captain carefully monitored the lee bow which sometimes began to disappear under the water before he carefully brought it slowly back with a soft but firm touch. The swells were coming from behind us now, and rather than confronting them, we flew over their backsides, white water jetting over us in thirty foot plumes, so that it was sometimes hard to see as we crouched behind the windscreen. "Sailin' by braille, Sam!" William yelled. "I'm feeling the helm. Now this is sailing!" I had never experienced anything so exhilarating in a sailboat. Uncle Charlie thought ten knots was a big deal, but we were hitting twenty-five at least, and with a reef in the main at that.

In spite of our considerable speed, Maui remained quite distant. It was impossible discern any individual buildings. From our perspective the view of the island wasn't any different than it had been in the nineteenth century. As I elaborated on this thought, a sudden shadow obscured the sun. William felt it at the same moment, because we both turned to look behind us. Simultaneously Double Barrel began to rise as if drawn upward by a mysterious and unfathomable force. In an instant we were looking down at the trough of a monstrous rogue wave; the lip towered above us. William said later that the onset of the wave happened so quickly he didn't have time to freak out. Instead he instinctively turned the boat at an angle to the face, and we streaked across it, surfing. We dropped to the bottom but our momentum carried us out of the grasp of the monster even as

it robbed us of our wind. We watched it disappear, quickly receding, a solitary giant that was
born of an unknowable confluence of deep pelagic
energies. In that thirty seconds a mishandling of
the boat would have left us buried in thousands
of tons of water. The Double Barrel would have
been crushed to splinters, our own survival very
unlikely. The four of us were mute. We let the sails
flap in the wind. It was difficult to digest what had
just transpired—the suddenness of it, so fraught
with potential disaster, and then our deliverance,
almost miraculous. Dave was the first to speak. He
turned to Will. "Nice touch there, brother."

We sheeted the sails and resumed our voyage.
Within minutes we realized that something was
very wrong. William remarked that the helm felt
heavy, and she wasn't responding in a lively way.
The boat had a leaden quality, and Will correctly
surmised that she was taking on water. He ordered
me to open a hatch and check the water level in
the starboard hull. Sure enough there was already
a foot and a half in the well and visibly rising.
Dave found a manual bilge pump and set to work,
but it was futile—we were sinking. The weight of
the water pulled Double Barrel down by the stern
so that her bows began to lift. Partially submerged
now, she began to go down quickly. Detritus from
the boat began to appear on the water. Bottles,
coolers, life jackets, swim fins, t-shirts, rubber

slippers, even a bag of weed escaped to the surface. A cheesy little Sevylor raft, a pool toy that you could buy in a drugstore, was tied to the tramp; it had served as a sort of couch. It proved to be our salvation. William cut it loose and threw it over the side. Seeing the boom swinging wildly from side to side in the still ferocious wind, he barked out "Secure the traveler!" Almost in the next instant it swung violently to one side, hitting Jonas in the side of the head. He fell unconscious in the cockpit which was filling with water. William dragged him up the steeply sloping starboard hull and threw him into the Sevylor. Dave and I were swimming by now, trying to salvage anything that could be of use. We recovered a bottle of water, a wetsuit vest, and most fortuitously, the flimsy oars that went with the Sevylor. The little raft was only eight feet long and couldn't accommodate the four of us. It was agreed that William, as the strongest, would man the oars. Dave tied the painter to his waist and swam a few feet ahead, while I hung on to the back with a single swim fin in order to steady us. Jonas lay prone, still unconscious, murmuring incoherently. The Double Barrel had slipped beneath the surface and seemed strangely at peace. Minutes before she had been wracked by wind and waves, in her death throes. Now she was quietly suspended in the transparent blue water, her sails undulating gently like a huge sea anemone.

We had asked too much of her; a fatal seam had opened and doomed our beautiful vessel. But we had no time to mourn the loss of a boat. Our situation was dire. There was no way of telling how badly Jonas had been injured, and there was nothing we could do for him. Our survival depended on an insubstantial child's play thing. William felt that our best hope was to try for the island of Lana'i. A notoriously powerful current ran in that direction. With luck we would be carried to Shipwreck Beach, a graveyard for ships but a welcome landfall for us. If the current deviated, as it sometimes did, we would be swept past Lana'i and disappear in the vastness of the Pacific Ocean. Will bent to his task, putting as much force as he dared into the plastic oars.

By late afternoon the wind had not yet abated. Our little raft rose and fell as twenty foot swells passed beneath us in relentless procession. Will had not stopped rowing for hours. He paused every so often only when Jonas threw up, pulling him into a sitting position to prevent him from choking on his vomit. After each episode Jonas would curl up and shake visibly. He was in the early stages of hypothermia. Dave and I were actually at an advantage because we were immersed in relatively warm water and not exposed to the wind. Soon the setting sun created deep, shadowed furrows on the surface of the ocean, dark valleys between the unremitting swells. Stars began to appear even before the orange glow on the horizon was extinguished. At the crest of a wave it was possible to briefly survey the heavens, even from my position. I easily identified Saturn and Jupiter and the familiar constellations of Scorpius and Sagittarius. The night sky was comforting, really, a familiar canopy that I had memorized under the tutelage of Uncle Charlie, for whom celestial navigation was a religion. The ocean, by contrast, was black, blacker than the night. In a moment it could consume us, and we would vanish without a trace. As the hours passed I began to accept the idea of dying, and even as I did so I was overwhelmed by the beauty of the cosmos. I felt pulled into the infinity of the universe, as if I were slowly dissolving into stardust. I began to hallucinate and wondered if I was experiencing a strange foreknowledge of my imminent death. I was resigned and very tired, but conscious enough not to loosen my grip on the raft.

William's hoarse voice snapped me back into my body. "We're getting closer to Lana'i guys." Indeed, its dark outline had grown noticeably closer. "I think the current is working for us." We had all disappeared into our inner worlds, but Will's expressed optimism elicited an attempt at banter. Our spirits rose, and Jonas had at least not gotten any worse. He hugged the wet suit vest to his chest and groaned. A bright light appeared above the horizon and began to climb. It had to be a helicopter searching for us! Hope faded quickly when I realized it was Venus, the brightest and most visible planet. Another hour went by and it was obvious that the raft was losing air. It had started to sag in the middle, and there was no way of re-inflating it. Our hope had begun to flag once again when William shouted in a parched croak that he saw a moving light on Lanaʻi—obviously a car. This was no hallucination; we were much closer now. A half hour later we could hear the distant boom of surf as it hit the reef. Ever closer we came until we could see white water, faintly illuminated, thrown skyward by the impact of the waves and ripped away by the wind. We had reached a critical moment. Safely negotiating the reef was our next test. If the raft was overwhelmed, it would be difficult to swim the unconscious Jonas to shore. Timing was everything. We had to choose a relative lull between sets to make our dash across the reef. We approached cautiously, listening, and then William cried out, "Go for it!" He rowed frantically, I kicked with all the energy I had left, and a modest swell lifted us over the coral. We had achieved the lagoon and, two hundred yards later, the beach itself. As exhausted as we were, a surge of elation was irrepressible. We carried Jonas to an abandoned fisherman's shack that was equipped with a cot and a sleeping bag. As Jonas began to warm up, he opened an eye and said, faintly, "Where am I?"

"In fucking heaven, Dude." It was David's attempt at levity, but we all laughed with palpable relief. We discovered four warm cans of beer and toasted our survival. Dave and Will set out for Lana'i City to seek help, a long walk in the middle of the night. They were actually happy to be moving and grateful for the warm summer air. I was left to watch over Jonas who began to revive enough to carry on a muted conversation. I described our ordeal, and mostly he just shook his head in response. When I had finished, he looked up from his cot and thought a minute before saying, "We could have died, Sam. I have to believe that God was watching over us." My uncomplicated response was a simple "Amen." Jonas was right. A complicated belief system was not required.

Dave and Will returned with a friend they had awakened. Jonas was checked out at the hospital—a concussion, dehydration—and we took the morning ferry back to Maui, looking like the castaways we were, without any possessions, wearing salt encrusted surf shorts and borrowed t-shirts, our eyes blood shot and wild. The ferry people took pity on us and didn't charge us anything which was good because we had no money.

Family and friends were overjoyed, of course. Our disappearance had made the nightly news. A Coast Guard search was called off. It took days to recover, and I used the time to record the event in detail. Lovely Laura was especially solicitous and kept us well fed. I basked in her sororal affection. Little Stryder seemed to understand the gravity of what had transpired and hung around his dad more than usual. This latest crucible had the effect of stiffening my resolve rather than weakening it. Our courage and fortitude were tested in extremis. We had relied on and trusted each other in a desperate life-or-death situation. I was ready for the challenges of the upcoming harvest. I have never regarded myself as a "tough guy" and didn't then, but after the sinking of the Double Barrel I felt inexpugnable.

It was a confidence that I would need in the coming weeks.

# CHAPTER XV

TERRA FIRMA! TO TREAD UPON THE SOLID EARTH, to hike again in the woods, the verdant forest, was a distinct pleasure. Most of the plants had silver hairs now; a couple had begun to form distinct buds. Except for the Frontier which had been planted late, any plant that had not declared its sex was eliminated. Only females now remained in every patch, flourishing in the absence of competing males. We still examined them carefully in order to catch the rare hermaphrodite, a plant that appeared to be female but would issue a male part capable of seeding the patch.

Even high up on the mountain the days could be hot, and we liked to take our lunch in a shady grove. We hashed over the sinking at length, Will refusing to assign blame to his beloved sailboat, saying that as her captain he never should have gone out in those conditions. "Pilot error" was what he called it. It was interesting to hear each individual's story, four unique perspectives. David said he kept repeating a silent mantra, "Please, Lord, don't let me be taken by a shark." I was startled by this, and William only commented that he hadn't wanted to worry me at the time, but, yes, the area was notorious for a thriving population of tiger sharks.

A philosophical discussion followed in which Will revealed that his primary motivation during our struggle was a concern for his family, especially in light of Tom's recent death. I had to wonder why anyone would ever get married and take on such a burden with all its inherent risks. "An excellent question Sam, for which I don't have an excellent answer. As you know, I am a sentimental person, and marriage is, perhaps, sentimentality in its most exulted or hyperbolic form. Well, the ceremony anyway. Then, too, it is an existential act, one which we enter into with a free will. To declare one's love for another in front of family and friends is a powerful statement. It's naked bravery and a touchstone that you recall in the difficult ensuing years. We saved ourselves in the ocean because we were stalwart, but pronouncing the vows, now that's brave."

David had been the best man at Will and Laura's wedding and he recalled the nuptials. "There wasn't a dry eye in the house, Sam. Fuckin' a, even

I choked up." He smiled at Will. "Our guy here is deeper than I first suspected. Of course the 'reception' was a barn burner. The party went on for days. Beaucoup beautiful women. A lot of Laurie's friends came over from Cali and just stayed. And nothing gets women going like a good wedding. Sub-parties blossomed over the next several weeks. Hey, remember the night of 131 margaritas? There was a place in Kihei, Sam, that featured one dollar margaritas and our bill was a hundred and thirty-one bucks. They tried to 86 us but they couldn't; there were too many of us. The party moved to the beach and people started taking off their clothes, skinny dipping by moonlight, body-surfing au natural. Damn, we used to have fun. And now, well, we are....boring." Dave paused as if he had just realized that for the first time. "And I'm not even married."

Jonas perked up. "Marriage can be seen as a component of spiritual evolution in which one abandons an egocentric mind set and by empathizing with another soul embraces the larger human experience. It might be a necessary step in the process of maturation."

Dave was less certain. "Why are there so many divorces then Mister Guru?"

"Well, some people aren't willing to accept the strictures of marriage. It's a test that many fail. Not every monk becomes enlightened."

William offered another insight. "Perhaps we are making too much of a simple biological imperative. I don't deny the transcendent power of love, but really how long does that last? What is it anyway? Titillation? Is 'being in love' the best predictor of a successful relationship? Perhaps other criteria should be given more emphasis, like intellectual stimulation or even a mutual hobby. No, the real problem is that marriage goes on for too long in the modern era. We are in deep space where few have gone before. Only a few hundred years ago you were dead at fifty. You lived in a mud and wattle hut or a hog pen, spawned a few kids, half of whom died of disease or malnutrition, never walked more than twenty miles from your village and then you were gone. You were grateful for your porridge and a few sticks of firewood. Your wife stank but so did you. Love was an invention of the Romantics, dilettantes with too much time on their hands who composed ballads and scribbled sonnets to their unattainable amours. Now marriage must continually re-invent itself. 'Love' is the bait, but you move on, you procreate, you defend your offspring. I can't imagine being married for decades, but it seems that the compact must necessarily evolve. Certainly the social mechanisms of the past have eroded; the church and society at large no longer buttress the institution. Oh well, I'm full of shit. In the end all you can say is that somedays it's great and other days it sucks."

Jonas took a hit off the joint before replying. "To me the only good marriage is one in which you enable your partner to become whomever he or she aspires to be. That requires a certain self-lessness and is the deeper meaning of love. Love isn't about being mushy; it is, to use your phrase, an 'existential' act. It's what you do, not what you feel. This is what is meant by the act of love."

This conversation made me think of my failed relationship with Naomi. Were we too cultur-ally dissimilar? She was a Jewish libertine, and I held many old-fashioned convictions—at least that's what she said. I had thought of myself as forward thinking and liberated, but she berated me for clinging to the "old paradigm" of relation-ships. Did she want to fuck other people? No, that wasn't the point she would say. She felt bound by my expectations, although when I asked her to be specific she would become vague, saying it was just a feeling. What I did remember was her volup-tuous figure, the full breasts with brown areola, the thick, erect nipples, the enticing trail of black hair that ran from below her navel to a luxurious bush. She would sometimes put a leg up on the arm rest of the couch, open her kimono and start playing with herself. I never failed to respond. But even great sex failed to buoy up the relationship, or even intellectual and political compatibility. Maybe there was a role for love. I had persuaded myself that I loved Naomi, but once I met Maile I realized that it wasn't true. There was no enchantment, no courting. I was in a sexual fog. If I ever did get to make love to Mai, I felt that there would be a spiritual aspect that would make it more than mere physical congress. After the sinking I felt that she held me in greater esteem. I was sure that she liked me a lot, but I hadn't revealed the depth of my own feelings. I would continue to be her mentor and hope that she would eventually regard me in a different light.

Our confabulation was suddenly interrupted by a faint buzzing sound that varied in pitch. Will held up a hand for silence and now there was no mistake—it was a helicopter. We quickly gathered our things and hid under a shelf of overhanging rock. Every so often one of us would emerge to check on the chopper's whereabouts. From audial cues it seemed to be flying very low, systematically checking out the area at a leisurely pace. After an hour or so it disappeared. Dave said that forward looking infrared or FLIR, was standard Viet Nam era technology, and now civilian agencies often employed it. "They can detect heat from fertilizer, or see any creature—pigs, humans, whatever. I saw it used effectively in combat. Obviously they are mapping out the mountain. The question is, who are they?"

We returned home that evening to a very upset Laurie. "A fucking helicopter buzzed our house! It terrified the animals. It was so loud I couldn't think and so close I could see a guy inside. Those motherfuckers! They worked the whole neighborhood; I watched from the deck. They actually hovered at times, no more than a hundred feet AGL. Susie called me and said she was taking the kids and leaving her place." Will gave her a long hug and then made margaritas.

"This happens periodically, Sam. I think they are hoping to find plants growing in someone's yard, but clearly it is an attempt at intimidation, an effort to terrorize the civilian population as it were."

"It seems outrageous. Can't you register a protest?"

"Protest to whom?"

"They are executing a warrantless search. You have fourth amendment rights."

"Not in Hawaii."

"It's hard to imagine that some straight people aren't also outraged. What would the Founding Fathers think?"

"We are a meek bunch, no doubt. Perhaps it's a legacy of the plantation era. Once you accept this bullshit it becomes the norm and hard to rescind. They get away with it because they can. This might happen elsewhere, but I've never heard of it. In California the cops pretty much restrict their searches to public land or at least the wide open spaces. Can you imagine the police trying to do this to a New England village?"

"So you think it's the local cops?"

"Yes, judging from the type of helicopter and lack of an identifying 'n' number. The feds wouldn't paint out the aircraft identification. It would be against Federal Air Regulations."

# CHAPTER XVI

In early August the deep heat of summer overwhelmed the Islands. Even in Olinda the nights were warm and sometimes uncomfortable when the trades stopped blowing. Laurie brought out the fans. By mid-morning it was too hot for even minimal outdoor chores. We made a couple of forays to the south shore to surf, but, as Will explained, the south swell on Maui was usually blocked by Lana'i and Kaho'olawe. Only a warning level swell could get through and they were rare.

We did get one, however. Will took me out to a break called Ma'alaea, and I still haven't quite forgiven him. It was, and is, a long, fast, hollow wall that breaks with unusual authority. He had surfed it in the sixties when he came over from Oahu to visit a Punahou friend whose family owned a home there. "Nobody surfed it then, Sam. This was before the condos were built. Imagine this place with only a couple of friends to share it with!" From the shore I could see that hardly anybody was making the waves. Someone might make a couple of sections only to be snuffed out by the next one. "They don't have the right equipment, Sam. I've busted out my old ten foot Dick Brewer semi-gun with a thick stringer and heavy glass. The idea is to turn from the top, trim and go. You need weight and momentum for this wave. The modern board is too light and too short." My board was apparently both, although Will had pronounced it adequate. I managed a take-off, but I was behind the wave and got guillotined. I was clipped by one of the fins, took the full force of the wave on my back, and had my shoulder rammed into the reef. Will was paddling back out when he saw me and made a face. "You're going to need some stitches, dude." I could taste the warm, salty blood that was dripping from my forehead. After the emergency room we returned home and medicated ourselves in the usual fashion. W's remark about "Frankenstein's monster" loose in the house didn't strike me as funny. I shouldn't have been out there; my native guide had failed me. "I'm sorry, Sam, truly. It's just that you never know what your limits are until you test them. Anyway, you are accumulating some great sea stories!"

# CHAPTER XVII

THE PLANTS BEGAN TO PROGRESS QUICKLY. Despite the heat their deep roots kept them turgid and thriving; most all were plainly budding. The occasional evening rain shower provided all the water they needed. We sprayed them with a water soluble sea weed product and carefully top dressed each plant with an organic fertilizer designed to maximize the yield.

One morning I branched off the main trail to check an area with Dave. He stopped suddenly to examine a small nick in a tree. "Oh, no, it's the fucking Slasher!" He explained that this unidentified individual had appeared in previous seasons. "We've never seen him, but he marks his trail with a machete. Since he only comes out in August, he must be a rip-off. He is obviously not very discreet, but at least we can tell where he's been. The ground based rip-off is just one more thing we have to contend with. They can't cover ground like the helicopters, but some of the locals are pretty savvy. They can always pretend to be hunting and that gives them license to carry firearms." Dave opened his day pack and pulled out what appeared to be the stock of a rifle. Contained inside it were a receiver, a barrel, and a small clip of ammo. He quickly assembled the parts. "It's an AR-7 survival rifle. Not much, only a .22, but it's better than nothing."

That afternoon we met up with William and Jonas and reported the intrusion of The Slasher. William had his own story to tell. "We were headed down the jeep track and were cautiously rounding a bend when we saw two guys in blue jump suits with lettering on the back. They were staring at something on the ground and didn't see us. We jumped back and went the long way round through the woods. I guess this area is getting hot. From now on we have to exit only by walking down the mountain, and we have to stay off the jeep trail at all times."

It was time to begin the search for a drying house where we could process the pot. Dave contacted Barbie, one of the notorious Hoover Sisters, who had a legitimate job in real estate management. She understood what was required—a spacious, private, up-scale residence that was invisible from the road.

What she found was perfect, an old plantation house

owned by a kama'aina couple who were planning to spend the fall touring Europe. We could take possession on the first of September. Aki and Koa agreed to go in on it, as did Jim, Tom's partner. Barbie consented to falsify W's bona fides in exchange for some cocaine. He charmed the old folks, of course, and the house was ours for three months.

After the interview we stopped to grab some beer at the Makawao General Store, when our attention was arrested by an odd couple who each had an expensive Nikon camera. They stood out front, apparently taking pictures of our quaint town. It was obvious that they also displayed an interest in photographing its inhabitants. William nudged me. "Look at those two. Probably newly arrived mainland haoles. They've certainly got expensive equipment." He stared at them for a long minute. "You know what Sam? I'll bet those are the narcs that Clayton warned us about. He's got the mustache, the polyester aloha shirt, and she's dressed like Haight-Ashbury. We should leave."

These various incidents made us increasingly wary. We abandoned the mountain bike m.o. and started to once again enter the woods pre-dawn. My time with Maile became a refuge, a welcome literary diversion. She surprised me one afternoon with a prefatory declaration. "Sam, you know how much I like you. You have been a good friend and a perfect gentleman, and, to be frank, my feelings for you have deepened. We do not speak of love, wisely, but we can acknowledge our truths." I was about to blurt out that I did love her when she continued. "I feel that in order to really know me you have to understand my culture, my family. There is so much that you don't know." I leaned in to kiss her, but she stopped me. "I'm going to take you out to Kipahulu to meet my grandmother, my tu-tu." I must have looked fretful. "Don't worry, she won't pass judgement on you."

The next day we made the long drive along Maui's north shore, stopping briefly at the Hasegawa General store for a six-pack. We passed the Seven Pools and turned up a narrow road that wound through lush vegetation before ending at a large clearing that was planted with mango, papaya, ulu, and avocado trees. Banana stalks were heavy with ripening fruit; clusters of colorful flowers were artfully scattered throughout. The grass was neatly cut, and a path of shells led to tu-tu's house which stood at the edge of the greensward. The property was immaculately groomed and yet gave the impression of nature only marginally tamed, like the best English gardens. The house itself was modest. The unpainted wooden siding was gray with age, and the corrugated tin roof certainly needed replacing. In contrast the window frames were painted bright red and the glass was sparkling clear.

I half expected to meet a stooped old lady, like Grandma Bingham. I was taken aback when "tu-tu" appeared at the door. She was tall and erect with a full figure that her mu-mu couldn't conceal. Her thick black hair, streaked with silver, fell down over her shoulders and breasts. She was probably in her late sixties but her face was strangely unlined. She gave me a penetrating look that lasted only a moment before she extended a hand and offered a warm smile. "Welcome, Samuel. Please call me Elizabeth." She and Maile embraced and we went inside. "I'm glad you two brought some beer. It will pair nicely with the lau lau that Auntie Mary brought over." She laughed at herself. "Please forgive my pretensions. I spent too much time in Europe, I'm afraid." Maile explained that her grandmother once had a career in the opera before deciding to return to Maui. Elizabeth continued. "You see, Samuel, I have deeper obligations. This land has been in my family for many generations, indeed hundreds of years, long before Kame-hameha defeated our chiefs. How we've managed to hold on to it is a story too long to tell at the moment. Perhaps that is my granddaughter's task." She looked at Maile as if an understanding had passed between them. "So I thank you for helping her. Words can have great power."

We finished our meal and the six-pack while listening to Donzinetti's "L'Elisir d'Amour." As the recording ended she turned to me with a wry smile. "I know what you young men are up to. Aki told me all about it. All that I would ask is that you be very careful about disturbing certain plants; respect for the forest is tantamount." It seemed like an odd request, but her firmness made it sound like a command. After chatting awhile longer about Maile's book, Elizabeth sprang to her feet with a movement so quick that it was almost incomprehensible. "I'm sorry to end our visit, but I have to take a little hike. Please do come back....both of you." Then she looked directly at me. "Maile is my treasure. Take care of her." I felt the full weight of my responsibility. Warmth and warning were commingled. We watched her go, springing like a deer up the trail behind her house. Her feet seemed to barely touch the ground. I was amazed.

"Where could she be going so late in the afternoon?"

"To a cave where the bones of our ancestors are interred—the na iwi. You see, Sam, she is a kahuna, what westerners would call a witch."

———

We returned by the dry backside of Maui, passing Kaupo before ascending to Ulupalakua on a treacherous, ill-maintained road. Across the formidable

Alenuihaha Channel, the Big Island of Hawaii loomed in a purple shroud of late afternoon light. I became contemplative, trying to process what I had just seen and heard. Maile turned to me. "Sam, my grandmother makes no secret of who she is, and yet it is something that we, her family, do not usually share with outsiders." I replied that I felt honored to have been introduced to her and asked if she, Maile, had ever been to the cave. "Grandmother feels that I am not yet ready. The mana of the na iwi is very strong. The cave itself is a lava tube high up the mountain in the wao kele, or forest, which Hawaiians believe is the interface between man and the gods. It is carefully hidden and has been for centuries. She will take me there someday."

"Does she intend to spend the night there?"

"Probably."

"That sounds kind of spooky."

Maile laughed. "Not to her. She is a kia'i, or guardian, and is perfectly comfortable with spiritual entities."

When Maile dropped me off I went immediately to my room and made extensive notes in my journal. I had been on Maui for a year, and yet I was just beginning to plumb the depths of my ignorance.

# CHAPTER XVIII

A WEEK LATER WE HAD ANOTHER BRIEF SCARE, this time from Mother Nature. A hurricane force tropical low was approaching the islands from the southeast, and we feared that it would decimate the plants. We spent a day cutting stakes and securing the plants with elastic garden tape. Although the sky was tenebrous and threatening, not a drop of rain fell, and the wind was calm save for an occasional eerie gust. Fortunately, the storm had veered west, sparing us, but it threw up the biggest south swell that anybody had ever seen. Almost forty boats were crushed on their moorings, and their detritus littered the shoreline for weeks. That was also the day that we cut our first early plant and carefully divided the branches in mock ceremony.

We made a town trip the next day and met Aki for lunch at Naoke's Steak House in Wailuku.

It was a masculine establishment that was frequented by politicians, contractors, fixers, union reps, and various underworld types. The portions were large and the high backed booths allowed for private conversations. As we entered the restaurant, four men at the nearest table gave us the once over. Aki was not the sort of fellow that anybody stared at for too long. A solid 240 pounds, he had put himself through college playing football for Oregon State. His long hair was neatly plaited and both biceps were adorned with tribal tattoos. He met the eyes of the men, and they turned away and resumed talking. The alert hostess seated us at the other end of the room. As Aki perused the menu he leaned forward and said, "I'm sure, William, that you recognize those gentlemen." Will replied that he did indeed know who two of them were, Makuakane and Chun. "The other two are Toguchi, head of Vice, in his civilian clothes, and Morisaki, the mayor's aide-de-camp."

"Do they know you?"

"Nah, they just give everyone what they hope is an intimidating look. You know, stink eye. It's the natural reflex of goons."

"It looks like they are holding a business meeting, and I'm sure it has to do with the upcoming harvest."

"No doubt." The waitress appeared at our booth. "I'm going to have the New York steak, rare, a baked potato, and a side of salad. Order for yourselves, my brothers, it's on me." The steaks were thick, juicy, perfectly cooked, and required numerous beers to complement them. As we left the restaurant we noticed that Makuakane's table was empty.

# CHAPTER XIX

WE TOOK POSSESSION OF THE DRYING HOUSE on September first. It had a spacious, well-ventilated attic that we accessed by cutting out a small panel in a bathroom closet. We strung strands of twine along its length and dedicated various bays to each partnership, an act of extraordinary optimism.

The house had a turn-of-the-century grandeur with its high ceilings, polished wood floors, large fireplace, a broad veranda, a built-in bar, and even a billiards room. It was tempting to turn it into a boys' club, but we had to be careful not to generate too much traffic.

By the first week of September the plants had matured more quickly than we had first calculated, probably in synch with the waxing moon. Will and I stood in the middle of Razor Ridge admiring our beauties, gently squeezing the buds to affirm their hardness, when a helicopter began to works its way down the narrow valley. It was so low that it actually passed beneath us in the defile. We could only see the rotor blades as it slowly passed by. After concluding that we hadn't been seen, Will looked after it as it made its way down the mountain. "That's a type of chopper that I haven't seen before, Sam. It's an old Bell. I wonder if it's a privateer. Maybe someone is going to go after the pot before Green Harvest. This isn't good at all." When we met up with Dave and Jonas that afternoon, they confirmed a similar sighting. Will made a pronouncement. "Let's take it all, everything. We'll have to leave the Frontier of course since it's weeks away, but everything else should go. Now. It's close enough." The effect was galvanizing. We leaped to our feet, grinning, and quickly assigned each other an area of responsibility. We reassembled hours later having completed our assignments. We all had thick plastic trash bags and rolls of duct tape. We cut the plants up in sections, leaving the plate leaves to provide a protective cushion for the buds. We taped each bag, heavy with pot, to our packs. I had so much weight that Will and Dave had to pull me to my feet. I staggered, a gelastic figure festooned with black plastic bags. Each of us was similarly burdened, and trekking up the mountain felt like we were climbing Everest, a step at a time.

We had to take the jeep track because slipping through the woods would have been impossible. I was in shape, but my legs burned with the effort. We were never more vulnerable. Deft movement was out of the question, and anyone coming down the road could have seized us and our harvest in one fell swoop. We had taken a break about three quarters of the way up, standing and stretching, when we heard a vehicle rapidly approaching from above. Instantly we dragged our packs off the road and hid behind a fallen tree as two jeeps bounced by, barreling down the mountain. It was already twilight, and we decided to wait until nightfall to resume our hike. As the stars came out our task took on a new urgency. We had to make a second grueling trip to get the remaining bags. Whoever the rip-offs were, they were going to be very disappointed. Dave thought it probable that they could only do so much at night and would have to wait until dawn to thoroughly canvas the woods, perhaps with airborne help.

When we finally achieved the top of the jeep track where it intersected with the EMI road, we pulled our booty into the underbrush and covered it with branches and leaves. The open question was "Now what?" The bags formed a hillock and obviously required a vehicle to move them, something we had not made an arrangement for. A quick conference produced a plan. William and

David would walk out of the forest reserve and down Olinda road to civilization. Will would get his truck while Dave borrowed a key to the gate from his friend. They would rendezvous and come back for Jonas, me, and the pot. Dave took out his AR-7 and admonished me to "Guard the pot. A round is chambered, just flick off the safety. And don't shoot us for chrissake when we come back." When they were gone Jonas and I looked at each other in disbelief. We were unlikely candidates for a shoot-out.

Hours passed. Moonlight filtered through the trees, casting long shadows. A pueo shrieked as it searched for prey. The wind rose and fell, moaning and then silent. Chill air slid down from the summit of Haleakala; the night was bright and cold. Somewhere around two or three in the morning we finally heard a noise on the road, but it didn't sound like Will's truck. We peered out of our hiding place and saw an old VW beetle—Laurie's!—with its tell-tale psychedelic flowers painted on the side. Will turned off the engine and said in a loud stage whisper, "The fucking truck wouldn't start. Start bringing the bags down." We stuffed them inside the car, taped them to the surf racks, propped open the front hood and stacked them there, even securing some to the rear bumper. Will could only steer by leaning out the window, while Jonas and I stood precariously on the narrow step rails, holding on to the racks for dear life. Dave cleared a space above the headlights and braced his heels against the front bumper, the rifle resting across his lap. "We're gonna owe Laurie something for this."

If there are miracles we certainly experienced one that night. We were a complete bust, a clown car of marijuana, yet somehow we made it to the drying house before dawn having encountered no traffic at all. In spite of our deep fatigue we hauled the pot into the attic and hung it all up. We were quietly elated and made a big celebratory pancake breakfast before crashing on the living room couches.

The next morning we were stirred by the crunch of tires on gravel. It was Aki in his lifted 4x4 Toyota truck. A carefully arranged tarp concealed his cargo. He burst in with his usual boyish enthusiasm. "Hey hey. Something smells good! Well we had some good fortune as well. Help me bring it in." We listened to his harrowing tale of harvesting under the gun. "Man, they were like angry hornets. I swear they were more vehement than usual." We quizzed him on the aircraft. "No Hueys, so it wasn't Green Harvest exactly. There was the yellow cop copter and a weird old fashioned looking thing. I didn't see any external loads of pakalolo hanging underneath either of them, so they were probably pissed off." We inquired after cousin Koa. "Oh....well, he is in mourning. See, he was following me out with half the pot in his truck, and at some point I realized he wasn't behind me. I turned around and found him throwing bags out of the bed of the burning truck. It seems that the battery bounced loose, severed the brake line, and ignited the fluid, setting the engine on fire. He couldn't stop, of course, without brakes, so he slammed the truck repeatedly into an embankment 'til he came to a halt. At first he ran, but then the thought of half our harvest going up in flames overcame him, and he dashed back, and that's when I saw him, a frantic figure illuminated by the flames. Anyway, he loved that truck, and now it looks like a burned marshmallow. I told him that our harvest would allow him to buy any vehicle he wanted, but I couldn't console him. I mean, you've seen it....rims, stereo system, custom paint....totally tricked out. So I told him to take the morning off."

The next day Will went to Fukishima's for groceries and the newspaper. The bold headline announced a helicopter crash in Kipahulu. The story said that two people were killed in the late afternoon accident, "an unidentified pilot and a passenger, Bertrand 'Biggy' Chun, president of

Atlas Security. A second passenger, Big Island rancher Lincoln Makuakane, is in critical condition at Maui Memorial Hospital." It was a shocking and not unhappy turn of events. We pored over the details, but there was little to be gleaned. Witnesses reported that the helicopter was seen flying earlier over the forest higher up the mountain, although the actual crash site was near the shoreline. The weather, according to people in the area, was "beautiful." The NTSB was dispatching a team to investigate the accident.

William thought that the crash would necessarily throw the local underworld into turmoil, but Aki wasn't so certain. "Somebody will step up. The Syndicate might even have wished it. Plenty young guys wanna move up. But for sure that will take time, and that's good for us. We gotta move a lot of shit." When I saw Maile that weekend for our "editorial conference," I mentioned the strange timing of the accident and hoped that her grandmother was not too upset by it. Maile looked at me with a level gaze that reminded me of her tu-tu. "Samuel, it was her doing. She put a curse on them."

# CHAPTER XX

"Y ou see, Sam, I live in two worlds. We
all do really. One is rational, academic.
The other is subconscious, mystical,
unfathomable to our narrow mental constructs.
Jung proposed that unless we acknowledge both
of those worlds we will be victimized by our ignorance. The professor in an ivory tower has a very
limited perception of reality. Likewise primitive
man was a victim of superstition. Maybe 'magic'
is simply a matter of paying attention to the world
around us, unlike the bullshit hocus-pocus 'miracles' of the priesthood. We all have powers that
we don't tap. Do some people possess magic, or all
the rest of us too lazy or ignorant to develop what
we have been given? These nascent faculties have
to be discovered, developed, nurtured, trained.
For that you need a teacher. My grandmother is
mine. I have a responsibility to her, and at times it

does feel like a burden. No, wait. There is more to tell. I have only spoken obliquely about my father and you never inquired. I told you that my mother died when I was young and perhaps you assumed that he had also. The truth is that he is in prison, Halawa, and was set up by Makuakane and Chun for a murder he didn't commit. He will get out soon. My grandmother was fearful of having her grandchildren involved in what could have been bloody retribution. She wanted to protect us. She was only waiting for the right time to take out Makuakane and Chun. Once they transgressed the boundaries of her domain, the area above her house, they violated a powerful kapu. It was her duty to kill them, for which she had to summon considerable mana. It is unlikely that Makuakane will survive his stay in the hospital. His is to be a slow death. You, Will, Dave, Jonas, and all the other pot growers are only the lucky beneficiaries of what she did. Now the score is settled."

# CHAPTER XXI

W E HELPED JIM HARVEST HIS CROP, AND AKI and Koa continued to bring in theirs. As the attic filled we became increasingly concerned about security. At various times one of us would pose as the estate's "lawn maintenance engineer," lingering near the entrance in order to intercept any interlopers. Aki was grumpy in this role, but Koa relished his disguise. I was indifferent.

The attic was nicely cross-ventilated and the September heat allowed the buds to dry quickly. When the pot was ready to process, it became necessary to hire a trimming crew. Laura, Rebecca, and Maile were obvious "captains" who worked the pot but also supervised others, and that was where the problem lay. Who could be trusted? A large team was required to to deal with the crop as quickly as possible, and yet every extra person posed an increased security risk. Each of the women had a trusted friend or two, so initially eight women sat at the table when the first trash bag of pakalolo was dumped before them. Trimming scissors in hand, they attacked the pile with amazing dexterity. Each had a large ziplock before her, and the raw material was transformed into nuggets of gold. They were well compensated, of course, since we wanted happy campers who felt included in the obvious bounty. We paid by either weight or an hourly wage, which ever option worked to the employee's advantage. Eventually the crew included as many as thirteen women, some of whom worked topless in the sub-tropical heat. It was always fun to reflect on all the marvelous variations of the human breast. Lines of cocaine were de rigueur, even for those theoretically opposed to the drug. Its use was easy to rationalize; the hundreds of pounds of marijuana had to be dealt with as quickly and efficiently as possible.

There was certainly a festive air at the "Big House" as we came to call it. The harvest was largely in, the women flitted about in various states of undress, there was an absurd amount of the best marijuana in the world, the old couple had a killer stereo system, the fridge was stocked with superior beer and champagne, and someone was always willing to whip up a big meal in the large, old-fashioned kitchen. The finished product was packaged in seal-a-meals and stored beneath the house in a compartment that had once been a wine cellar. It was easy to become complacent in those circumstances. After all, our chief nemesis was still in the hospital in critical condition. From Kaupo to the Westside most growers were having a pretty good year. Our serenity was dashed, however, when news of a big bust in Kula came in over the coconut wireless. A sudden gloom fell over our party. Apparently the Feds had raided a drying house with all the attendant drama they could muster. It was reported that more than a dozen men in flak jackets and armed with automatic weapons kicked in the door and herded the hippies around at gun point. Several were cuffed and the "evidence" was confiscated; a jilted girl-friend of one of the growers had ratted everyone out. The women had to endure lewd and offensive remarks, and a loyal pitbull was shot for his temerity. Aki glowered upon hearing the news and gave vent to dark mutterings about what he would do to any law enforcement officer who threatened a woman. His mansuetude concealed a volcanic temperament, and made the rest of us fearful of a confrontation with the Feds. He must have been a terrifying defensive end.

Will and I volunteered to go back to the woods and check on The Frontier, a series of patches further to the east that had been planted late. It felt good to be hiking again, and we were happily surprised to find that the plants were still there. A sizable bonus awaited us in October, and frankly we liked having a reserve sequestered in the forest.

That evening Rebecca appeared at the Big House gushing about having met the nicest couple at the Makawao General Store. They had accosted her as she carried a case of beer to her car and made discreet inquiries about the possibility of buying some marijuana. Will led the questioning. "Did you see their car?"

"Well, yeah, it looked like a rent-a-car. They were obviously tourists."

"An American car, say a Ford?"

"Yes, come to think of it—a full-size."

"What did you tell them?"

"I said maybe I could help them out with a little."

"You didn't mention large amounts did you?"

"Of course not! I've been in this business too long, Will, for fuck's sake. They're probably honeymooners."

"Gosh, Becca, no need to get huffy, but you know the saying, 'loose lips sink ships.' What did they look like?"

"Well, they were an odd match. He was kind of straight looking, actually, although he affected a mustache. His pants were creased! She, on the other hand, had a flowing skirt, peasant blouse, beads, Frye boots, and a flower behind her ear.

Very Bay Area. They said they were amateur photographers trying to 'capture' upcountry Maui."

"Did you arrange to meet them?"

"No, I just said that I'd look for them in Makawao."

"They're narcs, Becca."

"Narcs! How do you know?"

"I have a friend who is a Federal prosecutor. He gave me their description."

"Wow....they sure had me fooled."

"Deception is their profession. Fortunately they are not all that clever."

—

"This feels sophomoric at best."

"I grant you that, Samuel, but we have to do something." We had parked at the Veterans' Cemetery below Makawao and were walking toward town. The plan was for Will to distract the narcs while I injected super glue into the door locks of their car.

"There is always the possibility that this will only anger them and encourage them in their efforts to apprehend us."

"True, true. But a day without a car will certainly slow them down."

"And why do I have to do the dirty work?"

"Because of your choir boy looks, your innocent, Boy Scout aspect. Besides, I want to face the
enemy up close. Maybe I can learn something."
The car, a Ford Crown Vic, was parked at a distance from the store, and I was able to see Will
engage the narcs in conversation while I furtively
did my handiwork. I walked away quickly and
waited for Will at Piero's, sipping a cappuccino.
When he arrived he ordered a coffee, and we
waited for the fun to begin from the safety of our
observation post. Their attempts to open the car
were frustrated of course. It took them a few minutes to realize what had happened, and then they
began what looked like an animated argument. We
were too far away to hear the words, but they were
probably accusatory. The couple's gestures were
large and angry. The woman went to the pay phone
and made several calls. A second cappuccino later
a tow truck arrived and then another Ford with
tinted windows. The couple climbed in, slammed
the doors and headed down the hill to Paia.

"Well," said William, that was most satisfactory."

"They did seem to be upset, if that was your
goal."

"It was. A cop is one thing, but a narc is another.
They trade on people's trust. They subvert good
intentions to an unhappy end. That's the definition of evil. Anyway I kind of wanted to vibe
them in order to confirm Clayton's information.

I asked them about their photography, but they kept trying to steer the conversation around to marijuana."

"What did you say?"

"I said that I didn't smoke marijuana."

# CHAPTER XXII

THE WOMEN CONTINUED TO WORK FURIOUSLY. After a few weeks all the pot was dry and most of it had been trimmed. William and I were home, preparing to go to the Big House, when the phone rang. It was Clayton. "William, get everything out of your drying house. Now. The Feds are planning a few warrantless searches. Basically they are going to send a couple of undercover types to a number of suspect addresses. They will pretend to be looking for someone while, of course, casing the joint, looking for unusual activity, checking cars, and taking down license plate numbers. Above all don't let them in the house and escort them off the property. They might try to use the phone, a common ruse. You certainly know about the big Kula bust. That was done by the book, but they know that time is running out on the harvest season and they need better results."

"We are indebted to you, Clay. What about the local cops?"

"In the absence of Makuakane's leadership, the police are at odds with the Syndicate. The mayor has backed out of any involvement because he needed Makuakane's support to keep all the county agencies in line. Meanwhile the Feds are unchecked. They are aggressively pursuing information in order to justify their 'Hawaiian vacation' to grumpy Washington bureaucrats."

"You are good friend Clay, and we owe you something."

"Don't you dare send me money! But I will tell you, and keep this under your hat, I will be running next year for a seat in the State Senate. Contributions to my campaign fund will be greatly appreciated."

"I will be your most loyal supporter."

"You'll be in charge of shaking down our Punahou classmates."

"I look forward to it. I'll keep you abreast of things here."

We hurried down to the Big House and found everyone loafing about, smoking pot, listening to records on the magnificent sound system, and sampling exotic beers. With Will's announcement the household sprang into action. A big pot of coffee was brewed. We went up to the attic with a shop-vac and cleaned it thoroughly. We took down all the lines of twine and pulled nails out of the rafters. Downstairs every nook and cranny was swept; even the garbage was checked for roaches and anything pot related. Most importantly we had to address the pot itself which was still stored in the wine cellar. Jim opted to take his portion home where he had prepared a vault under a storage shed. The rest of us, Dave, Jonas, Will, Aki, Koa, and myself hatched a plan. We would rent a condominium in Kihei and store everything there in the short term until we figured out what to do. Once again I was the straight man, designated to present myself to the condo manager ("Sam, you have a Connecticut driver's license!") It was the off-season for tourists and he was glad for the business. As soon as he closed his office for the day, we began to ferry the pot down to Kihei in Koa's new surf van. It ended up filling an entire bedroom, or at least all the floor space if you included the untrimmed material in trash bags.

To finish the trimming, Maile, Becca, and Laura set up shop in the condo. In a few days they were finished, and it was time to contemplate our next move. Becca installed herself and her daughter in the Big House, a luxury for her, in order to keep an eye on things for the old couple who owned the place. I was elected to baby sit the condo owing, once again, to my wholesome appearance. The situation was tenuous to say the least. It was imperative to get the pot off the island and, ideally, to New York. We could have divided it, of course, every man for himself, since we kept careful records of who had so many pounds, but Aki and Koa had no local market, and David, Jonas, and I were pretty much dependent on Will's connections. Will didn't mind helping everyone out, but he was reluctant to accept responsibility for our collective fortune. The rest of us quickly decided that we would "kokua" Will four to five hundred a pound once the pot was sold in the city. Still the problem remained of how to get it there. Going back and forth with small amounts would only increase Will's exposure. It was Aki who came up with a solution. He had another cousin who was a freight forwarder for United Airlines in Honolulu. If we could get it there, artfully packaged, cousin Kawika could ensure its arrival in New York. Needless to say, he would have to be well compensated. A quick call to Kawika elicited a positive response, although he was somewhat taken aback by the amount he was required to handle. It was he who suggested that we pack the pot in large fiberglass fish boxes, seal them with a bead of surfboard resin, and slap a "fresh fish" sticker on each container. A piece of the puzzle remained; we had to get the marijuana to Honolulu. The problem took on a new urgency when Rebecca reported that the Makawao narcs had come by the Big House claiming to be looking for a friend. They recognized Becca and wondered if she had any pot for sale. She replied curtly that she did not, and that the Lymans, her employers, resented intrusions. They left disgruntled, their facade having slipped a bit.

Deliverance came from an unlikely source. George called the Olinda house and Laurie gave him our number at the condo. Will picked up but I could hear the Professor's booming voice through the ear piece. "Hey, boys! It's old George come to visit you guys on the fabled island of Maui!"

"George, you've caught us at a bad time. I'm afraid we're not in a party mode right now."

"Well....if that's the way you feel...." He sounded hurt from what I could hear.

"No, no. We would love to see you, it's just that we are in the middle of something. Just come on down. You'll see." Will gave him our address in Kihei and half an hour later he appeared at the door, a bottle of tequila in hand.

"Ok, what's so damn important that we can't have some fun? I want to go to Baldwin Beach and meet girls. Gurls, gurls, gurls! I'm tired of the Honolulu crowd." Bear hugs all around and then we led him to the back bedroom. "Holy shit! I can see what you're up against. What you have here is a major logistics problem, a problem that a lot of people would be happy to have. Good work!

Very good work." We found some ice and George poured each of us a tumbler of tequila. We sat at the dinner table and explained to him the necessity of getting the pot to Honolulu. The fish boxes were almost ready, but we didn't know how to get them to Oahu. "Let me see. I'm a master of logistics. Let me think. Hey, got something to smoke? Good, I should hope so." He rolled a joint and was about to spark it when he brought his fist down on the table. "Damn! I got it! Oh, this is brilliant! Fish! Fish you say? I'll go back to Honolulu and borrow Boy's 38 foot Bertram. Oh, that thing is tits—totally outfitted. I'll bring it back here, we'll load the boxes in the well, scatter some ice about, and have a leisurely cruise to Honolulu where we'll off-load at the commercial docks and store everything at the Suzukis' facility. Voila!" He beamed at us, and we had to admit that it was indeed a brilliant idea. Will did have to wonder, though, if Boy would go along with the scheme. "Are you kidding? He's indebted to you guys, and me. His old man has never been happier. The marriage gave him a new lease on life. Hell, the bride and groom are off to Vegas next week to gamble. Boy even said that if you guys come back to Honolulu, he wants to treat you right—penthouse suite, dinner at Michel's, high end hookers, the works. Borrowing the boat will be no problem. It just sits in the Ala Wai most of the time anyway."

"How soon can you be back? The Feds are breathing down our necks."

"I just got here! But alright, I'll fly back in the morning, organize the boat, and leave the following night. Passage should take about fourteen hours."

"George, you are saving our asses."

Since we couldn't leave the condo and all was decided, nothing remained but to finish off the bottle. The pot and tequila put George in a talkative mood. "This will be fun! I need a whiff of danger, of intrigue. I grade papers for a living, I have an office, I attend faculty meetings, I meet with department heads, I fill out forms, I write letters of recommendation, I suffer the complaints of mediocrities, I chair committees, I go to Christmas parties, I pretend to care about bureaucratic in-fighting—promotions, tenure, salary. I occasionally get laid by a grad student, I lend a sympathetic ear, I am pressured to publish, I am required to listen to the hand wringing fairies who are my colleagues. I hate academia. You guys are alive, you have a fuck-all attitude, a joie d'vivre. Adrenalin and fear course through your blood. And lust. For money, for broads, for adventure, for confrontation. I wasn't always a loveable old fart as you know. Embedded with those cats in Viet Nam, I knew what it meant to live on the razor's edge with the smell of gunpowder and cordite, blood, stale sweat, the stink of rotten flesh. I inhaled evil, embraced terror, found refuge in confusion, got lost in a cloying jungle, prayed to an indifferent god and defied his judgement. Oh yes! You can't put a stopper on the bottle. Good for you guys. Fuck the man. I hope you never fall prey to the tenter hooks of bourgeois existence. Of course, William, you have a family, so you have to watch their backs. So be it. Your wife is tough, the kid will probably be a warrior too. Of course I'll help you! I need to reclaim my dignity, my sense of self. I am getting old. My knees hurt. It's hard to tuck my shirt in because my left shoulder is frozen. A piece of shrapnel still rests against my spine. I should have a hearing aid but vanity won't permit it. I fumble for my reading glasses. My dick is becoming a phantom limb. I can't remember shit sometimes. Pot and alcohol numb me, make me insensate, but I can't suppress the sadness that threatens to overcome me. I'm not depressed though. At least not clinically. I don't want to kill myself. I just want out. I'm drowning in the mundane. I love my country and hate the people who run it. How do we grapple with them? We must resist, we must thwart them. They are rapacious. They are willing to destroy the planet in order to live in their gilded cages of gold veneer. We can't comprehend their greed. It is antithetical to our nature, our very souls. Oh yes. Let's get your pakalolo to Oahu, to New York. Liberate the tired, down trodden city-folk with this potent herb. You are lions guarding your kill. You only take what you need. The jackals would take it from you, but we will snatch it away." He paused for a minute to knock back another glass of tequila before resuming his rant. "Professor, indeed! Give me a mop and a broom. I'll be a custodian, a silent witness to bullshit. Redemption! Resurrection! I rise from the tomb of old age, the sepulcher of decay." Will and I shot each other worried glances. We had seen this kind of performance before, but George seemed a little unhinged. Suddenly, seemingly dumbstruck, he stood up and wobbled to the couch, where he stretched out and put a hand over his eyes. "Of course you'll give me a small cut, you wouldn't do otherwise, so I needn't mention it, but there's the dental work and shoulder surgery, just a little to wet the beak...." Soon he was snoring and Will gently covered him with a blanket.

We were all groggy the next morning, but strong coffee and a big breakfast helped to clear the cobwebs. Will reminded George of the plan he had concocted the night before. The Poet had recovered his professorial dignity and replied that he certainly recalled what he had said. Moreover, he stood ready to put the plan into effect. "I'm off to the aerodrome, gentleman. Just as soon as we smoke a doobie, that is. Hang tight by the phone, and I'll call you to update my progress."

When George had left we called Aki and told him to bring the fish boxes down that night. We slipped the containers into the condo under the cover of darkness and filled them with the neatly packaged contraband. Leaving room for ice, part of the disguise, we were able to fit fifty pounds into each box. We would add the ice in Honolulu and seal them shut before shipment to New York. When we were done we had a dozen units ready to go. Dave, Jonas, and Koa dropped by to admire our handiwork. At first we were mute with the enormity of our accomplishment, then Koa broke out a bottle of homemade swipe and proposed that we drink to our continued success. Everything now depended on George.

# CHAPTER XXIII

A COUPLE DAYS WENT BY AND WE HAD NOT heard from the Professor. Every passing hour added to the tension. Finally, and without preamble, he checked in. "All is in readiness, lads. I just had to organize a few things, but I'll be leaving tonight. Passage will be a little easier once the wind has died down. I'll call you when I've docked on Maui." With that cryptic but reassuring message he hung up.

The next morning he called from Ma'alaea Harbor to announce his arrival. We dashed over as quickly as we could, stoked that the plan was coming to fruition. We found George standing on the dock, but the 38 foot Bertram sport fisher was no where in sight. William was mystified. "George....where is the boat?"

"I told you that I had to juggle some things. See, Boy promised his mistress and her girlfriends a trip to Kauai this weekend. Fishing, partying, that sort of thing. He is as apologetic as all get out."

"What the hell?"

"Now, now, everything is taken care of. We arranged to borrow Papa-san's sampan." With a flourish he pointed to an ancient looking boat whose paint was noticeably peeling. We could see algae growing at the waterline. A strange sooty funnel rose above the deck.

"Oh fuck. You've got to be kidding me. That.... thing!"

George became defensive. "That 'thing' happens to be a very seaworthy boat. It got me here didn't it? Admire it, will you—the flared bow, the high gunwales, the sturdy construction. Nope, they don't make 'em like this anymore. You know I don't think you appreciate my efforts. If this doesn't suit your exquisite tastes...."

"I'm sorry, George, truly. Your efforts have been heroic. We are all appreciative. And did I mention that there is at least twenty large in this for you? That should take care of some surgeries." George was quickly placated and happily showed us the many features of the old tub.

"Now guys, here is the cool thing. This boat is the basis of the Mirikitani fortune. The old man fished this vessel for years and used the money to establish his other....interests."

"So, it's a bit of living history?"

"Stow the sarcasm. Besides nobody will question us in this boat. The Bertram looks like a coke dealer's fantasy. 'Hula Girl' on the other hand is a working craft. Furthermore, we can dock at the commercial wharf and avoid the gossips at the Ala Wai Yacht Harbor. No, this is perfect."

"You are absolutely right. I guess I was just looking forward to the panache of the Bertram. Not to mention the exhilarating speed, the luxurious appointments, the well stocked bar, the creature comforts, the expensive tackle, etc."

"Like I said, Boy feels terrible. His blonde bimbo coke whore mistress has got him totally wrapped. I have tried to counsel him on this matter, and he appears to understand, but then the next thing you know he's back in her clutches. It's a terrible thing to witness a friend being so pussy whipped, but what more can I do? Anyway, you will note that he threw a couple of cases of Dom in the well by way of apology."

"Apologies accepted. Time to load up."

That evening we conveyed the fish boxes to the Hula Girl in Koa's van. We congratulated the Professor on the splendid ruse that he had inadvertently conceived. We were fishermen and looked the part. George was fatigued from the previous night's voyage, so we decided to sleep on board in order to effect an early morning departure. Laurie and Stryder came down to wish us well. An avuncular George took a particular delight in encouraging the little tyke to clamber all over the boat while carefully instructing him in nautical terminology. He sat on George's lap and vigorously turned the steering wheel, shouting out imaginary orders. Laurie insisted on toasting our success, so we broke out a bottle of champagne. When it came time for her to leave, she and Will and Stryder hugged each other for a long time. A single tear rolled down her cheek. "I love you William. I always have. Vaya con dios." She waved to George and me and stepped off the boat onto the dock. I watched them go, hand in hand, mother and son. George, plainly moved, broke the silence.

"You have something special, William. Honor it."

The narrow bunks on board were meant to accommodate individuals of a smaller stature. After a fitful sleep we were up at dawn and made breakfast in the galley. An hour later George, now The Captain, fired up the ancient diesel engine, and we nosed out of the harbor, Oahu bound. It was a brilliant October morning; a single cloud clung to the slopes of Haleakala and the ocean was pure glass. We rose and fell off only slightly on a small, long period swell. "Hell, boys, we might as well fish for real!" Soon we had half a dozen lines out, and the lures danced along the mirrored surface. The splash of the bow wave, the singing valves of the engine, and the warm autumnal sun soon had us happily mesmerized. The worries of land grew more distant with every passing minute. We stood shoulder to shoulder in the wheel house and rolled a fat one. Will and I felt more relaxed than we had been for weeks. I looked back at the stunning beauty of Maui, and felt a quiet joy percolating within. This was the adventure of a lifetime. The Captain announced that he was going to nudge us a little bit in the direction of Lana'i, a slight alteration of course, since he was sure that we would find fish there. Will and I heartily agreed with the idea; it was funny that catching a fish seemed to take precedence over the greater mission, but then again we had no strict timeline. Aki wouldn't fly over until we had landed in Honolulu.

As we got closer to Lana'i we reminisced about the ill-fated Double Barrel and recounted our harrowing experience to George. "Well, boys, you can look at that one of two ways. Either your seamanship was utterly lacking, or it was masterful." He cackled. "Now, however, your old sea dog captain will guide you safely to shore; a veritable Ulysses I am." No sooner had he uttered this mild boast than the engine stopped running; a clattering noise was followed by utter silence. The tachometer fell from fifteen hundred to zero. We were dead in the water with six hundred pounds of Maui's finest marijuana in the hold. "Well what the fuck!" exclaimed our captain. Will didn't say a word; he calmly walked out to the bow and sat in a lotus position with his eyes closed. I knew from our long acquaintance that he only resorted to silence when he was really upset. "I guess it's you and me, Samuel. Let's go have a look at the engine." We did, and George was relieved to find that it required a relatively simple fix. "I just have to replace a broken belt, and we have plenty of spare parts." The belt was difficult to reach, however, and the repair would take a couple of hours. He decided to start the "kicker," a fifty horsepower Honda outboard that was deployed in the event of an emergency such as ours. We would head for Lana'i where it would be easier to work on the engine in the relative calm of the harbor. "Heading back to Maui is out. Lana'i is closer anyway, and above all we don't need the Coast Guard to come sniffing around. Go forward and tell Ahab that the situation is under control." I informed William of the good news, and he merely nodded. A few hours later we were tying off in an empty slip at Manele Bay. Will had lightened up and came back to consult with George.

"Brave Ulysses! We have foundered on a distant shore. What hope have we?"

"Why don't you boys get lost for awhile and see what mischief you can get into. I'm busy." We decided to take his advice and stroll over to the beach which was only a short distance from the harbor.

Although the beach was public, it was in the domain of the ultra luxurious Manele Bay Hotel which was situated above it. Will wanted to explore the property and told me what we had to do in order to successfully "penetrate" the facility.

"What you have to do, Sam, is grab a monogrammed hotel towel from one of the cabanas, fold it over your arm, assume an arrogant attitude, and boldly stride up to the pool like you owned it. Which you do in a manner of speaking, since you are a rich guest." Armored with towels we approached the pool area and were happy to discover a frothing hot tub. Our immediate companion was a woman in her fifties who had been retrofitted by a team of estheticians and looked the better for it. She wore one of those strange bikinis that you only see in Vogue magazine—a black affair held together by gold rings. The top barely covered a pair of pneumatic breasts.

"Well," she said as an opening conversational gambit, "where are you gentlemen from?" Will dispensed with desultory chit chat and countered with a basically truthful response.

"I, that is my crew and I, just arrived on my yacht."

"Really!" She sat up a little straighter and motioned for the pool boy to bring her another mojito. Will had plainly piqued her interest. "My ex-husband and I used to keep our yacht in the Med, but we found it so difficult to keep a good staff on board."

"Indeed. And servants can be so indiscreet."

"Wait! Haven't I seen you somewhere before?" She pulled her Gucci sunglasses down her nose with a lacquered forefinger, the better to take Will in. "Didn't I just see you in….yes, I know….with Meryl Streep. Oh my god…."

"Please, please," Will improvised, "we've come here to escape the paparazzi. Maui can be so…. confining." He laughed and urged her silence with a finger to his lips.

"Oh, I understand. You can be assured of my discretion." She paused. "Well, I hope that you and your entourage can at least come to the owner's party tonight. I'm told that it's the event of the year on this little island. Food and drink utterly gratis. And, who knows, perhaps there will be some willing company." This last speculative remark was delivered deadpan, although its lascivious intent was clear.

"My secretary failed to inform me, but my personal attorney and I will most definitely attend."

Will made a gesture in my direction. "My producer will certainly want to come as well. I thank you madam." After another half hour of pleasantries, we excused ourselves from the hot tub and headed back to the boat to inform George of our discovery. He had finished the repair and was relaxing with a cold bottle of champagne.

"I swapped out all the belts, and she's running great. Now why don't you lads join me in partaking of Boy's most excellent bubbly." Most of the bottle was gone, so we opened another.

"So dig this, Professor. There's a big party tonight at the hotel, free food and drink, all you can handle. It's a good thing that I threw some white linen shirts into the sea bag." The atmosphere aboard the Hula Girl had changed radically. A few hours before we had been morose; now we were happy pirates, intent on plunder. We all shaved and George and Will even trimmed their beards.

The party took place in a big, open air room whose massive doors were parted to afford a view of the ocean. We decided to effect our entrance through the pool area in case someone was checking names at the formal entrance. Shortly after sunset we made our way to the hotel, holding our topsiders in hand, pausing to wash our dirty feet in the pool. Tanned and fit, we had dressed down fashionably in our slightly faded Levis and elegant linen. I can say immodestly that we were rather dashing in a dishabille sort of way. As we burst onto the scene, heads turned and a murmur ran through the happy crowd. Almost immediately a waiter appeared to take our order for top shelf margaritas, while another offered lobster tail canapes. A superb trio of Hawaiian musicians held forth in a corner of the great room which was lavishly decorated with antique Asian art.

We had ordered a second round when our new friend from the hot tub appeared and took Will's arm in hers. "There are some people you just have to meet," she trilled. "Oh, and should I introduce you as Jeff or Jeffery."

"Well, um, I'll let you choose. Either will do, I'm sure." She laughed gaily in response, and I began to wonder who exactly William was being mistaken for. It didn't seem like the right time to ask, though. A good fisherman knows when to set the lure and then pay out a little line. The crowd had apparently been alerted to the presence of a Hollywood luminary. I tagged along, curious about the outcome.

"Jeff, I want you to meet the manager, Richard Kleindale."

"I'm so happy to meet you," he gushed. "I'm a huge fan; I love your work. And rest assured, your privacy will be respected, although some of the ladies might want an introduction." He winked, one man to another. "Now tell me, is everything to your satisfaction?" "Jeff" replied in the affirmative, noting only that the hot tub was merely lukewarm. "Oh, I'm so sorry. I will make a note of that." An assistant pulled out a pen and pad. "You see, tonight we are reviewing the twenty million dollar renovation that we just completed. This affair is a sort of coming out party. Mr. Murdoch himself might show up this evening." William expressed his astonishment.

"Twenty million? But the décor is so....gauche, not to say tacky, mind you, but sometimes understatement can be a more powerful expression." Mr. Kleindale was crestfallen, and Will realized that in his candor he had been an impolite guest. "I am sure, however, that the public will admire it," he said with a reassuring smile. We excused ourselves, feeling a little bad. Our self-appointed hostess was unaware of Kleindale's distress and giddy at the prospect of Murdoch's possible appearance.

"Do you know who he is? He owns this island."

"Yes, a regular Prospero," remarked William dryly.

We joined the crowd that had gathered around George who was holding forth in a loud voice, enjoying his new found celebrity has a Hollywood producer. Because of his occasional gaucheries, it was easy to forget that the Professor could be a charming and learned raconteur, especially when he had not overly indulged in alcohol. Another woman, wearing a red dress with shocking decolletage, thrust herself upon William, who seemed to enjoy the view. In a few minutes it was open season, and a covey of females was clustered around "Jeff." I was cornered by a southern California real estate developer who wanted my legal opinion on easements. I eventually made my escape to the opulent bar. The party was bubbling along nicely, a cheerful fantasia, when, emboldened by drink, I slipped the Hawaiian trio a twenty and easily persuaded them to play a James Brown medley. Now the pleasant affair was ratcheted up a few notches, and the rich folks loosened up considerably, dancing like the college kids they once were. When the food ran low, I went back to the kitchen and urged the staff to find some more. As the formal event came to a close, the hard core party goers adjourned to the billiards room upstairs where our money was no good; people vied for the privilege of buying us drinks. William slipped out with Red Dress in the direction of the hot tub, as I began to swoon. My last clear memory was of George running the table against a crabby looking old man who was swearing vehemently.

A chiming clock woke me up. It was three o'clock and there was not a soul to be seen. George and I had fallen asleep on a very comfortable couch, and management had graciously decided not to disturb us. "Get up guys. The party's over." It was William, grinning like the Cheshire cat.

"So it would seem," I replied. "I don't feel so good." We roused George and staggered back to the Hula Girl where we laid out soggy sleeping bags on the foredeck.

"Well, Jeff," said the Professor with a smirk, "how did you like being a movie star?"

"Ok, I guess. I never found out who I was supposed to be. That woman was voracious. But here we are, a bunch of Cinderellas, after the ball."

"At least we made a lot of money."

"What do you mean?" George pulled out a thick wad of bills. "Where did you get that?"

"I won it off that little wanker at the billiards table, Rudy Murdick or something. He doubled down every time he lost. You each get a share for setting up the con." He started counting out the money. Will protested that we hadn't set up a con. "Sure you did. Don't contradict me. A yacht! All that Hollywood bullshit. Oh, that was good!" We tossed and turned for a couple of hours before the first grey light of dawn ended our fitful rest. George fired up the old engine and we eased into open water. I felt a little nauseated, but Will and the Professor were full of mirth. "You know, boys, we should go fishing more often!" Hula Girl was headed for Oahu.

# CHAPTER XXIV

WE HAD TO HEAR, AT GEORGE'S URGING, W's tale of being seduced the night before. "She fucked me in the hot tub and then on a chaise lounge by the pool!" George pounded on the steering wheel, laughing so hard he almost choked.

"Ho, ho, ho! The Sirens lured Ulysses and his men, they were nearly entrapped, but they escaped, ever mindful of their quest!" Strangely my sympathies were with the cuckolded husband. I did not suffer from the constrictions of married life or the promiscuous possibilities available to a mature single man. No, I was in love, that dread and wonderful illness. Actually I did feel quite ill until I puked over the side. George and William hooked up the stereo system and sang along to a Beach Boys' tape. It was difficult for me to remain grumpy as the islands caught the morning sun. The weather continued to be perfect and the Hula Girl threw a long, undisturbed wake on the glassy surface. After a couple of hours my companions decided to take an overdue nap. They spread out beach towels and were soon sound asleep, leaving me at the helm. I steered us out of the Au Au Channel and into the Kalohi Channel between Lana'i and Moloka'i, paying attention to the Professor's final admonishment to "take her easy, 2000 r.p.m.s tops." When they awakened, we were off the south side of Moloka'i, churning steadily along. George pronounced that it was "beer-thirty," and popped some cold ones to go along with the sandwiches he had made.

Will took a turn at the wheel while George rolled a joint. "So I guess you young scofflaws got a break when Makua and Biggy went down in the chopper." He said this with a wry grin; Will pretended to take offense at the characterization. I chimed in, remarking that we were aided by a powerful witch whose curse had been their downfall. I regretted mentioning this almost as soon as I had said it. The Professor looked at me as if I were daft. "That's good Samuel. Now please back up that assertion with some empirical evidence." I told him in great detail about Maile's grandmother and what I had witnessed. He smiled. "No doubt the curse, as you call it, played a significant role. But I must tell you that a little bird told me that a certain someone had a bolt loosened on the main rotor assembly the night before the fatal flight." Who, we wondered, had the audacity to take such a bold action? "Someone who took umbrage at Makuakane's attempt to muscle in on his gambling racket and who had an undisclosed financial interest in one of the helicopter tour businesses and therefore access to the flight line. That's who."

"Boy?" guessed William.

"All I can say is that the Lord works in mysterious ways, and the curse is as good an explanation as any. Let's go with that." Our estimation of Boy rose considerably. Like many sons of a rich and successful patriarch, he was a pudgy figure, somewhat indolent and overly indulged, although certainly affable and well mannered. In light of this new revelation, he was cast in a more favorable light. Now Boy was incisive, devious, and even dangerous.

"A toast to Boy!" cried William who raised his beer can. We joined in, although I could not discount the contribution of Maile's grandmother.

In the afternoon we were in the Kaiwi Channel with Koko Head plainly in sight. The wind had finally picked up, but remained less than fifteen knots. We rocked and rolled with the quartering swell. Soon Diamond Head lay ahead, and as we rounded that famous landmark the early evening lights of Waikiki came into view. A few miles later we were abeam downtown, and then we made our turn into the harbor and Hula Girl's berth. Our timing was perfect; all was quiet on the wharf. George called the Suzukis from a pay phone and a few minutes later a white commercial van pulled up driven by a trusted nephew. We unloaded the fish boxes and drove to the familiar safety of the nearby processing facility. The sisters greeted us warmly and tittered excitedly about their small role in conveying a load of marijuana to New York. "You boys so naughty! I guess we naughty too!"

William called Aki to tell him that we had arrived in Honolulu at last, and Aki flew in the next morning. He got in touch with his cousin and arranged for our shipment to leave that night on a red-eye to JFK. Will and I went to a downtown travel agent and bought two first class tickets on the same flight. Aki agreed to depart a little earlier on a different airline. He was just too outsized, too conspicuous, to travel with us. Besides, he didn't own the requisite sports coat. But he wanted to keep an eye on his property, and, I suspect, to have a fun time in the big city, having heard Will's ribald tales.

Late that afternoon we threw ice in the boxes for camouflage, sealed them with surfboard resin, and affixed "fresh fish" stickers. Aki drove the cargo to the airport while William and I prepared for the long flight. We bought suits, shirts, ties, and footwear at Liberty House and presented ourselves to George who confirmed that we passed inspection. "Well, well, a couple of Ivy League businessmen returning from a little romp in the Islands. Going back to Wall Street to sell billions of dollars worth of junk bonds." After dinner he drove us to the airport and bade us a fond farewell. "Stay in touch you desperadoes. Maybe I'll fly out to New York to collect my twenty gs. God speed. You were always my favorite students." After manly hugs all around we boarded the airplane. I had only flown first class once before and remarked to Will that a fellow could get used to it, as a very interested flight attendant poured us flutes of pre-flight champagne. If indeed there is a tide in the affairs of men, we were riding the flood, or at least we thought so. We clinked our glasses and then froze as two tall men in dark suits with ear pieces appeared at the cabin door. Each had a short list in hand, obviously a passenger manifest, and they carefully scanned us as they slowly made their way down the aisle. They stopped to give W and me a hard stare....and then moved on. Returning to the front of the first class compartment, one of them turned and allowed Rosalynn Carter to come aboard. It was the former first lady's Secret Service detail, a protection to which she was still entitled. The rush of adrenaline that we experienced would last for hours, unmitigated by a cornucopia of champagne. The flight was anti-climatic after that. It is hard to imagine now, but the meals en route were splendid, and we were well-served by the flight attendants who insisted that we look them up in the city. I suppose we really did look like high rolling bond traders. In those days, too, the back of the aircraft was basically a cocktail lounge. We spent several pleasant hours drinking with a famous rock band that was returning from an Asian tour.

Upon landing it was a little difficult to switch gears and confront the task that lay before us. JFK was a humming hive of businessmen, bewildered foreigners, frazzled families, college kids, hipsters, frightened looking old folks, and the occasional rich couple looking faintly disgusted by the hoi polloi surrounding them. It was a jostling, frenetic, stir-crazy mob getting sucked into the maw of that relentless city. We joined the exodus to the curb, waiting our turn for a cab while inhaling the poisonous exhaust fumes that had displaced the air. Chauffeurs held signs aloft, hotel shills worked the crowd, gypsy drivers sized up potential victims, while would be thieves searched for the unguarded piece of luggage, all under the watchful gaze of a couple of cops who idly twirled their billy clubs. Our Pakistani cabbie was unhappy when we told him we were only going to United freight but was quickly satisfied when Will gave him two twenties.

By design Aki had arrived earlier and had already loaded our shipment into a rented van. Rather than being fretful, he was as excited as I had ever seen him. His grin was contagious. "Oh man, what a great flight! I got three phone numbers without even trying! I said I was a Hawaiian chief going to a United Nations conference. This place is alive with possibilities. There's even a Hawaiian group playing this weekend in midtown, wherever that is, and I went to Kam with one of them!"

Driving into Manhattan at rush hour demanded Will's full attention, and it was a sobering experience. By the time we arrived at the Gramercy Park Hotel we were all utterly exhausted. The valet assured us that the hotel had its own parking garage, and that our vehicle would be perfectly safe. The Gramercy was the hotel of choice for many touring musicians, so the staff had seen it all, but our little group caught their attention. The assumption was that William and I were big time producers and that Aki was our bodyguard. We didn't challenge that surmise, and each of us took a separate room. We had dinner at a sushi joint on 17th street and discussed our strategy. William confessed that he hadn't spoken to Madeline in awhile, but he was sure that she would contract for most of the load, although it might take a couple of weeks to move it all. This made me a little uneasy since it was obvious that we couldn't keep all the pot in a parking garage for very long. Will agreed, but the first step was to get in touch with Madeline.

The next evening we made a quick call and took a cab to the West Village. George's success at the billiards table was still evident as Will pulled out a roll of twenties. Lana'i, the hotel, the boat, the party all seemed very distant, as indeed they were. Aki had elected to seek out his pal from high school on the promise that we would take him to Maddy's at a later date. We were greeted warmly but were greatly disappointed to learn that Madeline was abroad, consulting with her banker in Zurich. Rather than returning immediately to New York, she had scheduled a holiday on St. Barts. Z had been left in charge in her absence. When we told him how much we had brought with us, he expressed astonishment and seemed a little flustered. "Really, William, you should have called a couple of weeks ago. In her absence M left me with a very limited budget. I could do twenty pounds tomorrow, but, my goodness, you're talking over a million dollars even with a deep discount for volume. But let me mull this over....I think I can help you out to a degree if we can make a couple of hundred a pound, or let's say, five percent of what you negotiate with the character to whom I will refer you. Does that sound good?"

Will agreed that was more than fair. "Very well. Why don't you two go downstairs and enjoy the soiree—a couple of supermodels are there—while I make a phone call or two. I must tell you, though, that you will be entirely on your own. Madeline does business with this guy periodically, and nothing has ever gone wrong, but he works out of Williamsburg in Brooklyn, a neighborhood so menacing that even the cops won't go there. And, to be clear, he is black. Calls himself Othello." A half hour later Z summoned us back upstairs. He gave Will a piece of paper with a phone number on it. "Call this number three nights from now at exactly ten o'clock. He'll give you instructions then. Meanwhile I'll see you tomorrow, and we'll do the twenty pounds." We thanked Z and headed back to the Gramercy. It wasn't all that late for New York, and Aki wasn't in his room. We ordered something from room service and discussed our strategy. Will and I worked well together, our relationship in the marijuana business having begun in college. Clearly we had to immediately find a secure place for our pot. A parking garage in Manhattan was much too vulnerable. We considered driving it out of the city to New Haven and bringing back a little at a time on the train. At least there we could park in a Yale lot and keep real eyes on the van. We considered that option for awhile, and then I remembered that my cousin

Lowell lived in the Fireboat House on the East River. I had last seen him at a family reunion four years before. We had gotten along well enough, although he displayed the narrow arrogance typical of Harvard graduates. The problem as I saw it was that they lived within the provincial confines of sleepy Boston, while we Yalies were drawn like moths to throbbing, crazy New York. In any case he was Uncle Thad's oldest son, and we had known each other since infancy. I was sure that he couldn't refuse us a place to stay for a few days. I called him and was pleasantly surprised at his warm response. Of course I didn't mention the hundreds of pounds of marijuana that we would be bringing with us.

The Fireboat House was an interesting structure. It was built in the 1890s to service the fireboats and their crews that cruised the East River as a sort of first line of defense against any conflagration. It stood at the end of a long pier that thrust out into the river and was equipped with bedrooms and a kitchen. Lowell and his friends were managing its restoration. An old investment banker had secured a grant to fund the project. Conveniently, it was situated right below the Gracie Mansion, the mayor's official residence. I say conveniently because the cops assigned to guard the mayor had been alerted to expect us and waved us through the gates. We were directed to park just above the Fireboat House; our pot was now guarded by the NYPD. Lowell and his buddies were gracious and pleased that we had brought with us a little authentic Hawaiian paka-lolo. Interestingly, they were all world class white water kayakers and kept their craft on the pier. Lowell explained that we were located directly opposite Hell's Gate, where the confluence of flood tides and river currents could sometimes produce treacherous rapids, perfect for making practice runs. Examining the cold, black water we could only admire their fortitude. Will and cousin Lowell were soon engaged in an animated conversation about the dangers of rough water generally, while the other two Harvards and I cooked steaks on the outdoor grill.

William and I had agreed that it was best to keep quiet about the contents of the van. We explained when asked that we were helping some of Will's classmates move out to Brooklyn, and that we would be in the metropolitan area for awhile. An imaginary wedding was to take place in Greenwich in a couple of weeks. Lowell seemed delighted by the news. "Could you guys stay here? We need someone reliable to watch over this place so that we can compete in Germany. I hope you can. We just have to clear it with Mr. Beecher, our patron. Spend the night and you can meet him in the morning." We didn't have to hem and haw, it was the answer to our prayers. Lowell thanked us profusely. The next day the pink faced old Wall Street veteran appeared in a proper blue blazer and regimental striped tie—a lanky, somewhat stooped gentleman crowned with a thatch of snow white hair. It was no surprise that he was a Yale alumnus. We spent an hour talking with him about our mutual alma mater. He was particularly interested in the benefits of co-education, wistfully recalling the era of road trips to Vassar. It was quickly settled. We received the imprimatur of the good Mr. Beecher, and in two days became the sole occupants of the Fireboat House. We quickly established good relations with the Irish detectives who were the literal gatekeepers.

Aki was informed of our new address, but he had already moved in with a dancer from the Hawaiian show. With the thousands of dollars already in his pocket from our first sale to Z, Aki was living large. The bearish brown man had integrated himself with a cohort of Island ex-pats and by extension a whole world of musicians, actors, and entertainers. One night we visited him at the show and watched his beautiful new girlfriend perform. "Guys," he said, leaning in over the music of the band, "there's more aloha here than in Hawaii. Look at this crowd. Any kine people, all digging it. Man, I love New York. Maybe back home we have the luxury of self-imposed segregation, but here everybody's packed in together, twenty-four seven. It's hard to maintain prejudice." He pulled out a roll of bills and summoned a willing waitress. "Bring us some drinks with an umbrella. Like Waikiki." She smiled and flirtatiously accepted a twenty dollar tip. We told him about our upcoming meeting with Othello, and he said that he would be happy to go along as "muscle," but Will thought it would be better to keep a lower profile. "Well, you guys know best. You know where to find me, and I have your phone number." When she had finished her hula, the radiant Haunani sat down at our table. Aki fairly beamed with delight.

# CHAPTER XXV

W E CARRIED A SAMPLE POUND IN A BATTERED
valise that we had purchased from a
bum. William regarded our trip to
Brooklyn as a lark and felt that at the worst we
would be ripped off for a little pot. I was considerably more wary. We decided to take the subway
since no cabbie would drive us to Williamsburg
anyway. Walking to the nearest station exposed
us to the city in the full throes of a Friday night.
Homeless men slept on heating grates, undisturbed
by the incessant noise of car horns, rumbling
trucks, sirens, animated conversations, tipsy men
in tuxedos singing in harmony (ex-Whiffs?), or the
occasional scream rising above the general din. A
whirlwind of trash mixed acrid exhaust fumes with
the smell of cooking oil from a falafel stand. A pan
handler in rags pushed his shopping cart full of
detritus with fierce determination while another

peed furtively in the shadows. Loafing hard hats from ConEd surrounded a steaming manhole, oblivious to the boisterous shouts of the bridge and tunnel crowd. Music drifted out of a club, offering no comfort to a lost, sweat-stained tourist couple lugging their baggage. What mysterious force held these millions together, what cohesive bond, what unknown valence? We were in the midst of moving, coursing humanity on a warm autumn night. A half moon, un-intimidated by the lights of Manhattan, insisted on her eminence in a world of artifice. William correctly read my thoughts. "I bet, Sam, that you are thinking how can anyone survive this mayhem? Or live here willingly? And yet it speaks to the human condition, the adaptability of man, his voluntary acquiescence to an invisible order. Look at them—all trying to look good, hoping to get laid, counting their money while they stifle their dreams. These people need our pot, Sam. They need to be liberated, if only for a short time." A nervous black man passed by, uttering "smoke, smoke" under his breath. When Will stopped he pivoted and trotted back to us, hoping for a sale. Instead William reached into his pocket and gave the dumbfounded man a beautiful Maui bud. We walked on. "Hey, Sam, the dude is a foot solider in the marijuana wars."

We changed trains in lower Manhattan and boarded a rattling old subway whose occupants thinned out considerably as we approached our destination. We were unarmed, relying instead on costumes of leather jackets and black fedoras and a "don't fuck with me" demeanor, although we didn't have much of an audience. We got off in a desolate part of Williamsburg and began walking through an area of abandoned buildings and deserted factories. The occasional streetlight threw a pool of light; the click of our boot heels on the pavement was the only sound. It felt like we had stepped on to the set of a film noir. We followed our directions and after a few blocks came to a large warehouse without having encountered a soul. Will pressed a buzzer, and a minute passed before we heard a freight elevator descend and stop. A large black man opened the door wordlessly and gestured for us to step in. Upon exiting we had to pass through several heavy doors that our escort opened with his set of keys. We emerged into a vast room that had probably been the main floor of an old factory. The original oak floors had been re-sanded and varnished. Thick candles flickered along the wall where they had been mounted. At the far end of the room a figure remained seated behind a large desk, flanked by a nubian guard of two tall men, black in the shadows. African masks adorned the wall behind them. The effect was intentionally theatrical. If there was a protocol, we didn't know what it was. After a few moments the stentorian voice of "Othello" filled the room. "I understand that you have something to show me." It seemed like a command. I turned to gauge Will's reaction and saw his jaw drop in surprise. He muttered something under his breath and took a few tentative steps forward. The bodyguards assumed a defensive posture; one reached under his jacket for his shoulder holster.

More clearly William said, "I would know that voice anywhere." Then "Othello" jumped out of his chair and peered intently at Will before bounding around his desk and striding briskly to the center of the room. The bodyguards looked at each other in confusion and then belatedly lurched toward the two men. "Thurman! Is that you?"

"William? Wild Bill? When Z described you, I was hoping it was you!" The two men embraced and held each other at arms length. The tension in the room dissolved in a moment as the former classmates regarded each other fondly. "We have some catching up to do. Allow me to introduce my two brothers, K'wane and Martin." There were firm handshakes all 'round. "And Samuel, I do remember you as well." Thurman had made an indelible impression on me when he appeared in the title role of the Yale Dramatic Association's production of "Othello." As one of our star basketball players, he had the regal stature required for the part as well as a voice that fronted a popular soul band. When Will chided him about his nom de guerre, he laughed and said that he was just trying to have a little fun. The five of us retired to a sanctum sanctorum behind the main hall, and Thurman broke out a two hundred dollar bottle of single malt Scotch whiskey. As we relaxed Thurman told his story.

"After graduation I tried Wall St., believe it or not. Firms were anxious to hire 'people of color,' but I quickly realized that there would always be a glass ceiling for us. Imagine me in a board room of white folks!" He chuckled at the thought. "But I did meet a lot of people with easy money. It was no problem raising some capital. At first I dealt everything. A lot of coke. That's how I met Madeline. But I soon realized what drugs were doing to our community, how many brothers were being ravaged, ruined. I resolved to only deal in marijuana, which isn't as profitable, but I can do so with a clear conscience." He paused and topped our glasses. "Most of the pot is Columbian, some Jamaican, some of your better Mexican. We can run smaller boats right up to a dock here in Brooklyn." Will wondered about the law and how much scrutiny Thurman faced. "That's the cool part. Nobody wants to come out here. Actually the neighborhood is pretty safe in that nobody lives here, really. There's some light manufacturing, but everybody leaves at five. Law and order, as it were, is kept by the Black Knights, a black motorcycle gang that operates out of an abandoned building. They tinker with their bikes by day and race them at night against other outfits for big bucks. The streets are a great race track; there isn't any traffic at all." I wondered if Thurman worked with them. "Oh, they're my eyes and ears. I told them to expect you. You were being watched. You see, I sponsor them. That is, I buy them the latest and hottest bikes, factory tuned in Japan. You should see the new Kawasaki. A bat out of hell."

We talked for hours. Martin had graduated from Columbia several years before and was now thinking of medical school. K'wane was on a leave of absence from Wesleyan and was about to travel to Africa. We inquired after Thelma, their mother, and Thurman told us that he had set her up with a high-end soul food restaurant in Harlem. He in turn was fascinated by our tales of Hawaii and the lengths we went to grow pakalolo. He had sampled "Maui Wowie" a couple of years back but had been unable to locate a source. "Madeline wouldn't tell me, and damn it was you all along! How ironic is that?"

Finally, after our long "talk story," it was time to get down to business. Will showed Thurman the pound. He opened the zip lock, stuck his nose in the bag, closed his eyes, and inhaled deeply. He smiled and picked out a red-green bud which he gently broke apart, allowing the aroma to fill the room. "Mmm....hints of pine, citrus, and rose." He rolled a joint and then carefully roasted an end, nursing the glowing ember with small, carefully calibrated puffs. When it was burning evenly, he savored the smoke and passed the doobie to Martin. "Man, that's good weed. What I like especially is the effervescent, energizing high. Madeline knows good marijuana, that's for sure. She'd only sell me a couple of pounds every year. And to think it was Wild Bill all along! Damn." Will told Thurman how much we had brought to the city, and he let out a low whistle and laughed. "Shit, man, I want it all for myself. Seriously, though, I can move it, no problem. Everybody who buys large amounts of Columbian wants Hawaiian for themselves and their select clientele. But I'll have to move it fifty to a hundred pounds at a time. I know you sell it to Madeline for twenty-eight, but I'm gonna have to get it for two. Next guy will put two to four hundred on it, etcetera. Know what I'm sayin'?" I looked at Will, and he nodded.

"Thurman, old friend and esteemed classmate, it's a deal. How soon can we begin?"

"Tomorrow night. Bring over an initial fifty pounds and I'll have a hundred grand for you. Now I don't want to be nosey, but are you keeping your stash in a safe place?" William explained our situation at the Fireboat House and told him that the stash was, in fact, being watched over by the

NYPD. Thurman's eyes widened and he let out a hoot. "That's the craziest thing I ever heard of! Man oh man. Ok. I'm going to have Martin drive you all back to Manhattan in my limo, and I'll see you manana."

That night we decided to sleep outside on the pier. It was still warm in October, and we lay in our sleeping bags and listened to the rush of the water beneath us. The skyline of the city loomed behind us, but its noise was barely audible. On the river the movement of lights marked the boats working the waterfront as they had for hundreds of years. To the north an arcing bracelet of twinkling jewels revealed the span of the Triborough Bridge. I was still very high, but I thought Will had managed to fall asleep when he said, "Sam, I know this isn't profound, but these same stars are watching over our home in Hawaii." Yes, I realized, it is my home too.

Dawn came early. It was a cloudless, perfect Indian summer day on the East Coast. A vast high pressure system hung over the whole corner of the continent. The sun was brilliantly reflected on the rippling surface of the river. We were making coffee in the galley when we heard the throb of diesel engines and then a shout. "Hey there! Yo! Up and at it! Somebody tie us off." We stepped out on to the pier and grabbed the lines thrown to us by a small Coast Guard vessel. We secured the lines to some cleats, and several crew members, bright-eyed and trim, jumped off. "Where are the guys?" asked the young lieutenant. "We dropped in for coffee." I explained that I was Lowell's cousin, and that I was in charge while the kayakers were competing in Europe, but, not to worry, the coffee was up and the bagels were warming. Introductions were made and the crew piled in. The lieutenant explained that they were frequent visitors and expressed admiration for Lowell's skill in running Hell's Gate. I asked if this was a regular patrol. "Oh yes. Someone's always in trouble. A tug will break down, a tour boat will hit something, some rich Jersey guys will get fishing line tangled in their props, a barge will break loose, and the other day we rescued a couple whose canoe had capsized. Where the hell did they come from? Last month we had to help a lost baby seal. Of course there is always the occasional dead body. You name it, we've seen it. And lately there are rumors of drug smuggling, which is hardly surprising. Apparently some of these wise guys use beat up old boats for disguise, while the more brazen employ cigarette boats, like the Miami Vice tv show." Will and I silently absorbed this information. When the crew had finished their breakfast, I invited them to come back any time. The cheerful young men wished us farewell and disappeared up the river.

"Well, Sam, we obviously have to alert Thurman." That night we loaded up fifty pounds in the van and drove to Brooklyn over the Williamsburg Bridge. Thurman was as excited to take possession of our pot as we were to take his money. To celebrate we uncorked a bottle of vintage Dom. Thurman received the news of the Coast Guard patrol with equanimity.

"In this business we have to guard against complacency. I guess it's time to alter our routine. Usually the Colombian is off-loaded in Hoboken, and we run it over here in a non-descript tugboat. We have our own dock, a remnant of a once vibrant Brooklyn waterfront. I am, by the way, buying up all the real estate I can in this area. I believe gentrification is only a matter of time." It was hard to imagine at the time, but Thurman's foresight would make him wealthy. "I am diversifying as quickly as I can. My goal is to be legitimate. The wheel of fortune is always turning, and the only constant is change." He then expressed concern at our having so much cash to deal with and recommended a downtown bank that would secure our money in a safe deposit box. "Remember Hodges, the swimmer? He's the branch manager. Tell him I sent you. Oh, by the way, it would be nice to tip the Knights a little, say a grand. Lester is the main man. He'll be out front." We left the neighborhood with a modest escort of motorcycles who left us at an imaginary boundary.

The next day we got a call from Aki who complained that Haunani was wearing him out. He needed a brief respite and opted to join us at the Fireboat House. Although he was pleased that our business was going well, he seemed preoccupied with his love life. "I don't know, you guys. She's half local, half New York. The show's over at midnight and then it's party time. We went to a place called the Palladium and stumbled out at dawn. Frankly, I'm exhausted. The bruddahs in the band like to smoke pakalolo, but I didn't tell them why I'm here." We were happy to counsel him, and the garrulous Hawaiian proved to be a big hit with the Irish detectives who guarded the Gracie Mansion—and us. Within a day he had procured free tickets to the show for them and their wives.

While we waited for Thurman's next order, we decided to throw a modest party. Haunani came, of course, bringing with her two lovely maidens from the revue. The guitarist and an ukulele player came as well. For the hell of it we also included Z and a few hangers on from Maddy's. As we greeted the girls at the gate, Detective O'Reilly gave us a big grin and a sly wink. "Curfew's at midnight. Only kidding, lads! Ha! Ha! Have a good time." It was as romantic an evening as I can ever remember. Hawaiian music drifted over the East River on a soft, star filled night. A tug tooted its horn in response. The Coasties stopped in for an hour ("Just coffee, please."), and the detectives dropped by in turn during their breaks. Later, Will and I took Lei and Ocean out on the water in a rowboat. Nobody wanted to leave, and they didn't have to; there was plenty of room in the bunkhouse. Lei was a willing sex partner, and I can honestly report that I didn't keep track of William, although Ocean and he were most affectionate in the morning. I certainly had fun, but, sentimental fool that I was, I couldn't help thinking of Maile. I missed her, her alert intelligence, her athleticism, her quirky sense of humor. I wanted to show her New York and marvel at her discoveries. I envied W's ability to compartmentalize his attachments. I never doubted his sincerity when he called Laura and told her that he loved her. I never questioned him in this regard, but he knew what I was thinking. He would laugh off his infidelities, saying they were only peccadilloes, and that he was, after all, taking enormous risks for his family and needed to let out a little steam now and again.

By noon, when the last stragglers had left, we received a phone call from Thurman. "One hundred, gentlemen. Same time tonight." Aki decided to accompany us, determined to see more of the "real" New York. "Othello" and he got along famously, talking at length about the demands of collegiate sports while piling up beer cans on a table between them. The talk turned serious as they discussed the African diaspora and cultural dissolution in general. We heard the term "white bwana," and they turned to us grinning. William told them to go fuck themselves and demanded a beer.

When business was concluded Thurman stood up at the stroke of midnight and announced that it was time for the races. The Knights were to be pitted against a club from the Bronx, the Skulls. The course had been cordoned off in the unlikely event of outside traffic. Representatives from both sides functioned as observers to guard against infractions. Not wanting to be mistaken for mere bystanders, we threw in five grand on the first go-round, betting on our guy Lester and his Kawasaki. At the drop of a flag, the combatants took off in a cloud of blue exhaust smoke and burning rubber. Even at a distance we could hear the scream of the big four strokes being pushed to the limit. We were rewarded when our man crossed the finish line three lengths ahead of a Skull mounted on a Honda. So it went for more than an hour, and by the end we had made out pretty well. We left a generous gratuity at the Knights' clubhouse.

# CHAPTER XXVI

W E BEGAN TO ACCUMULATE QUITE A BIT OF money. Aki was content to be on a modest allowance, and William and I were reasonably careful with our expenditures. Will kept strict accounts, remembering that we still owed George twenty grand and Aki's cousin ten. There was also the five percent that we paid out to Madeline's gang for the Brooklyn connection. We checked in with Dave and Jonas, and they were thrilled by our success and very comfortable with the numbers. We mailed each of them a box with ten thousand dollars as a small down payment on their shares. They were conscious of the risks we were taking, and we knew that they would kokua us when we returned home. For their part they harvested the Frontier without complication.

Pleasant October days rolled by. We visited the famous art museums, took in the latest movies, caught great music in the clubs, and ate very well at night, often accompanied by Lei and Ocean who always created a stir. We even took a train one Saturday up to New Haven to watch Yale crush Princeton in the Yale Bowl. Madeline returned, beet red from too much Caribbean sun, and helped us out by buying pot for the West Village regulars.

During this time our friendship with Thurman and his brothers deepened. One night we took the limo up to Harlem to meet the matriarch and dine in her upscale restaurant, Soul Kitchen. William and I were the only white people there, but everyone there was unfailingly polite. Of course we were the obvious guests of the majestic and formidable Othello. The staff was especially attentive to Aki who had pronounced himself an expert on ribs, or at least the consumption thereof. He devoured plate after plate, ceremoniously licking his fingers after each round. He went back to the kitchen to praise the chef and had an animated conversation with him about how to properly imu a pig. Over desert and then a digestif, Thurman said that we might be entertained by observing his Colombian operation at close hand, and suggested that we accompany him and his brothers later on. We readily agreed since we had become bored with New York nightlife. A little adventure seemed like the perfect tonic for our ennui.

We drove back to Williamsburg and changed into working clothes. K'wane brought an old tug down from City Island and tied up at Thurman's dock. "Giamatti Bros. Towing" was crudely painted on the side. In dirty slickers and watch caps we looked like a working crew. Aki looked especially piratical with his hair braided in a long pig tail. We passed under the Brooklyn Bridge, rounded the tip of Manhattan at two in the morning and took aim for Hoboken. The Statue of Liberty regarded us impassively, but she prompted a derisive comment or two from a few crew members whose ancestors had not been afforded the luxury of Ellis Island.

Thurman explained the delicacy of the upcoming exchange. The freighter, of Panamanian registry, was Colombian and manned by a notorious gang of pistoleros. They trusted no one and worked through a Puerto Rican agent who facilitated every sale and transfer. Thurman was only one of several customers, each of whom had an assigned time slot. He was fairly fluent in Spanish and used an encrypted radio to communicate with the "mother ship." K'wane throttled way back as we approached the decrepit shoreline of Hoboken. From a mile away the small freighter was barely visible, illuminated only by a single deck light. Thurman spoke into his microphone and waited for a response. There was none. He quickly ordered K'wane to begin a slow turn away. He tried to raise the Colombian ship a second time, but once again received no reply. Another minute passed as we began to blend back into the inky darkness of the Hudson River. Thurman scanned the receding shoreline with a powerful pair of binoculars but saw nothing untoward. He was about to initiate another approach when we heard the pop and crack of what sounded like fire-crackers. Muzzle flashes revealed the source of the noise; a firefight was taking place on the freighter. As we merged deeper into the protection of the night, Thurman kept a running commentary on the action. "There's another small boat tied up along side. They seem to be exchanging gunfire.... one man down....now two. Holy shit. Let's get the hell out of here, but slowly. And throw that fucking radio overboard. It would look suspicious if we were stopped and searched." Martin did so and made sure the five hundred grand was deeply buried in a locker belowdecks. In another instant the dock was brightly lit up by a hovering police helicopter. Flashing lights began to converge from all directions. Even at a considerable distance we heard the roar of twin 454s as the banditos ignited the engines of the cigarette boat. After some more sporadic gunfire, they were off. Thurman followed the action. "Jesus, they must be doing seventy or eighty knots already! No running lights of course. And wait....what's this? It looks like the Coast Guard is in pursuit." We heard a burst of machine gun fire and then a voice over a loudspeaker demanding surrender. "Good luck with that," intoned Thurman. Two minutes later we could still hear the faint rumble of the escaping boat, now well down the Hudson. Back at the dock the flashing red lights of the cop cars shimmered on the black water as the chopper continued to hover.

We were silent for some time as our own engines throbbed away like beating hearts. It was obvious that our night had almost come to a disastrous and premature end. When the adrenalin had subsided and it was clear that nobody was going to board us, Captain O issued a ration of grog, that is a shot of tequila followed by a beer chaser. Aki downed his and began laughing, a basso profundo that rose from deep within. He shook his head, unable to stop. "Oh my," he finally blurted out, "I frickin' love New York!" His laughter became infectious, a welcome release of our tension.

Back in Williamsburg our reflections were more circumspect. Thurman summed it up. "We could have been killed, robbed, or arrested. All bad options. I suppose we were lucky. I still have my money, but obviously I'll have to find a new connection. At least I'll be able to buy the rest of your pot."

We were dropped off at the Fireboat House shortly after dawn, looking somewhat bedraggled. "Ho, ho, ho!" exclaimed Detective O'Reilly, full of good cheer even at such an early hour. "Look what the cat dragged in! I hope you two had a good time. You look a little worse for the wear. How are the hula-hula girls treating you? Don't do anything I wouldn't do." We did our best to match the detective's up beat mood, but we were dead on our feet and in desperate need of breakfast. No sooner had we made coffee than we heard the now familiar cries of our Coast Guard friends. "Hey, hey! Lively there! A little help. Tie us off." The animated sailors jumped on to the pier, in vivid contrast to the exhausted figures before them. Lieutenant Jensen was still visibly excited after their recent adventure. "Whew boy, what a night!" I offered to make pancakes for everyone while the young officer gratefully accepted a cup of coffee. "You guys won't believe this, but we were involved in a shootout in Hoboken. Just hours ago! A small freighter was docked there, apparently with tons of marijuana aboard. As we approached gunfire broke out and a cigarette boat made a getaway. That thing could haul ass!" His admiration was frank. "Showed us nothing but wake and then—poof!—vanished, gone down river. We gave up at Sandy Hook."

"I got to fire the machine gun!" a pimply

seaman happily chimed in. The lieutenant ignored this outburst, and Will pressed him for details. Did he know anything about the rip-offs? Any clues as to their origin or affiliation?

"No, nobody gave us any details. Headquarters just told us to intercept the freighter. They must have been tipped off by the cops or the DEA. The cigarette boat was a surprise." We could learn nothing more about the camisado and changed the subject. After a long nap Will called Thurman to arrange for the sale of our last hundred pounds. The mood that night in Williamsburg was noticeably downbeat. Thurman announced that this buy was to be his last.

"At least for awhile. The wise man knows when to quit or at least enter into a period of quiescence. The events of last night were a clear portent." When he analyzed his assets, he realized that he was already a millionaire, at least on paper. "It might be time to go straight." He shook his head and then smiled. "But what will I do for excitement?"

William was consoling. "Maybe we should all grow up a little bit....or take up skydiving or something. I have a family after all." Aki entertained the thought of becoming a professional wrestler, and Martin decided positively to pursue a career in medicine. As for me, I was motivated to return to law school. The past year had provided enough dare-devilry to last a decade, if not a lifetime. A leather bound chair in the law library now seemed rather appealing. When the sale was completed, Thurman uncorked a bottle of champagne and proposed a toast.

"I quote from Shakespeare, gentlemen.
'With mirth and laughter let old age come,
And let my liver rather heat with wine
Than my heart cool with mortifying groans.'
Here's to the future and our friendship. Cheers!"

# CHAPTER XXVII

THE NEXT MORNING WE PROMPTLY TOOK A CAB downtown and deposited another 200k in our safe deposit box. In a private room we took out the cash and stared at it. It was a moment of complete triumph and sort of anti-climatic at the came time. We dutifully ran the numbers: 500 lbs to Thurman at 2,000, minus 50k for Madeline's commission. One hundred to same at 2,400. Then there was the payout to George and Aki's cousin, 30 grand in total. "Sam, I don't think anyone would object to our pulling out ten thousand for our expenses. So there you have it. One million, one hundred fifty thousand dollars." A lot of it was in bricks of twenties; it made for a big pile.

"If there was any justice in the world, we would give a handsome chunk to cousin Lowell. He's returning from Europe next week. On the other hand it's probably just as well that we keep him in the dark. I would hate for word to get out to the rest of the family. We can just take him out to dinner."

"I agree. Mum's the word. And Samuel, I sure as hell am not going to be responsible for everybody's money. You know what? Let's take out another fifteen out for the party."

"The party?"

"I've been thinking it over. Dave, Jonas, Koa, Jim, George—they're all going to have to come here and get their money. I'll figure each person's share. We'll send them all first class tickets and book one and all into the Plaza. Laurie and Stryder too. And Sam, we'll reserve a room for you and Maile."

I protested. "Really, William, that would be terribly presumptuous of me." I was flustered. "She might be offended by my forwardness. We are friends, but I really don't think she is interested in me in that way. She could have anybody. I amuse her, but in the end what am I but an ignorant haole?"

"Do you love her?"

"Well...."

"I know you do."

"Yes, well,....yes. I do, very much."

"Then when we get back to the Fireboat House you are going to pick up the phone and invite her to New York. It's time, Sam. You've been mooning over her for over a year. Right now you are at the

height of your powers. You have to trust me in this.
I've seen the way she looks at you. If you don't call
her you are a fool beyond measure."

Back at headquarters I took a shot of tequila
and then another. I placed the phone in front of
me. Ten minutes went by. Will pretended to busy
himself out on the pier. I took a deep breath. My
finger remained poised, inert, and then I did it. I
dialed her number. The voice at the other end was
distant and attenuated.

"Hello?"

"Maile, this is Sam."

"Hi, Sam. How's the big city?"

"It's good. Things are going well." I sounded
so inane. "Mai, I don't know how you'll take this,
but I want you to come to New York. I'll buy you
a ticket and put you up in the Plaza; it's a famous
hotel." There was a protracted silence.

"Will we have separate rooms?"

"Whatever you want, I just…."

"That's not what I want! Book us into the best
suite they have, you moron." She laughed. "Oh,
Sam, I've wanted this for a long time. Send me the
fucking ticket."

And so it was that the whole gang assembled in

New York. We went to Broadway plays, ate Italian, consumed copious quantities of champagne, and took a limo everywhere, courtesy of Thurman. In late October the first chilly night was a harbinger of the coming winter. The money was divided, and it was time to return home, to Maui. Maile and I had fallen in love; William, Laurie, and Stryder had renewed their deep affection for one another; George took a leave of absence from his academic duties and was cavorting with an old flame; Aki and Haunani announced their engagement; Jonas, Dave, Koa, and Jim were enjoying the roguish delights of the city and decided to stay awhile longer.

On our last night together, the crew rented a couple of carriages for a ride through Central Park. We nestled under the blankets and swigged champagne from the bottle. Maile looked angelic in her woolen shawl. Laurie hugged Stryder close and pointed out the mantle of stars above. "See those stars, Stry? Those same stars are watching over our home in Hawaii."

# EPILOGUE

IF, DEAR READER, YOU HAVE STUCK WITH MY TALE thus far, you are probably curious about how life turned out for its various characters. I did go back to law school as the third oldest student in my class. My career path was obvious. I was a public defender and then opened my own practice in criminal defense specializing in (what else?) marijuana law. My romance with Maile faltered after a year. We just had things we each had to do, separate destinies. She is now a professor of Hawaiian Studies at UH. We still exchange Christmas cards that always include a heart-felt note. I have kept in touch with Will and his family. I manage to get out to Maui every five years or so, and I am always shocked at the amount of change that has occurred in that relatively short period of time. William is remarkably unchanged, however, although age has calmed his tempestuous nature.

Laurie is a "silver fox," still beautiful and gracious in her sixties. They have a flower farm, but Will stubbornly continues to grow pot ("Legally, for fuck's sake! With little yellow tags!"). They had a daughter late in life, and she is in college. Stryder is a successful contractor with children of his own. Aki weighs three hundred pounds, and Haunani and he live on the family land in Kipahulu, surrounded by countless children and grandchildren. Dave got a college degree through the VA and teaches high school. Jonas fancies himself a guru and has a devoted following on the various social media. George passed some time ago, and I flew out to Hawaii to help Will scatter his ashes off of Waikiki. Thurman and I still occasionally have lunch at the Yale Club in New York when I am down there on business.

All the pot growers in this story kept at it for some time, a few for many years. They followed a cycle of boom and bust, but never had a season as glorious as the one I have described. My experiences of that time are certainly distant now, and I don't think I will accidentally betray anybody's closely held secrets. If you pried a little, you would find that many of the old timers have similar stories. We escaped to Maui for a variety reasons; many stayed. When I returned to do a little research for this book, I was struck by the number of complaints I heard about the difficulty of making a go of it on that storied island. I can only be amused; they have no idea. Perhaps now they will.

Samuel Elihu Bingham IV

'fini'

CPSIA information can be obtained
at www.ICGtesting.com
Printed in the USA
FSHW021115090321
79300FS